Silvia Vecchini - Sualzo

# A DIFFICULT THING

## THE IMPORTANCE OF ADMITTING MISTAKES

**FOR ABLAZE**

Managing Editor
**Rich Young**

Editor
**Kevin Ketner**

Design
**Rodolfo Muraguchi**

Publisher's Cataloging-in-Publication data

Names: Vecchini, Silvia, author. | Sualzo, artist.
Title: A difficult thing / Silvia Vecchini ; Sualzo.
Description: Portland, OR: Ablaze Publishing, 2021. | Summary: Every child makes mistakes and must deal with and admit those mistakes. This two-tone wordless comic shows how powerful the word "sorry" is.
Identifiers: ISBN: 978-1-950912-43-8
Subjects: LCSH Apologies—Comic books, strips, etc. | Apologizing—Comic books, strips, etc. | Graphic novels. | BISAC JUVENILE FICTION / Comics & Graphic Novels / General | JUVENILE FICTION / Social Themes / Emotions & Feelings
Classification: LCC PZ7.1.V425 Di 2021 | DDC 741.5—dc23



10 9 8 7 6 5 4 3 2 1

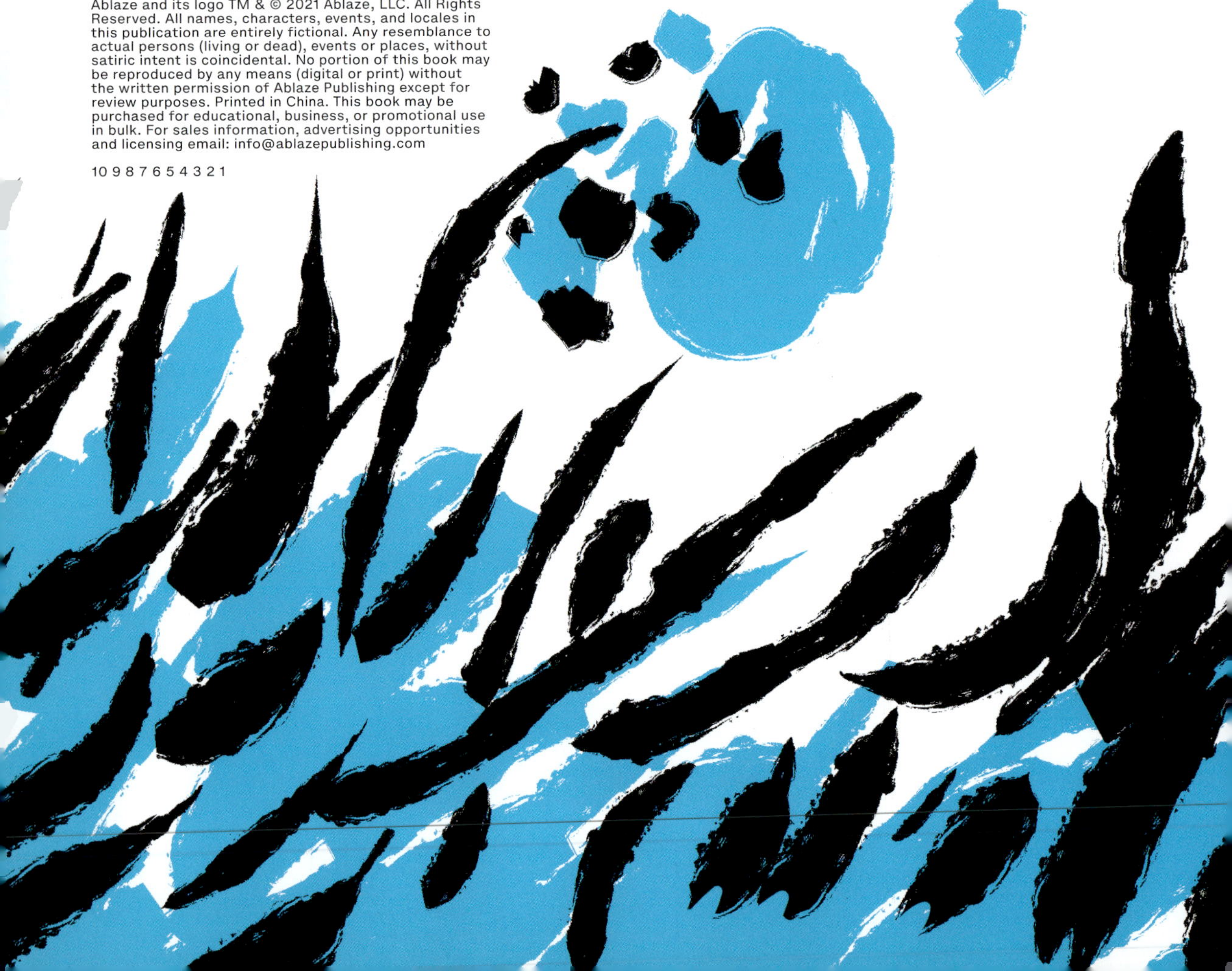

Silvia Vecchini – Sualzo

# A DIFFICULT THING

## THE IMPORTANCE OF ADMITTING MISTAKES

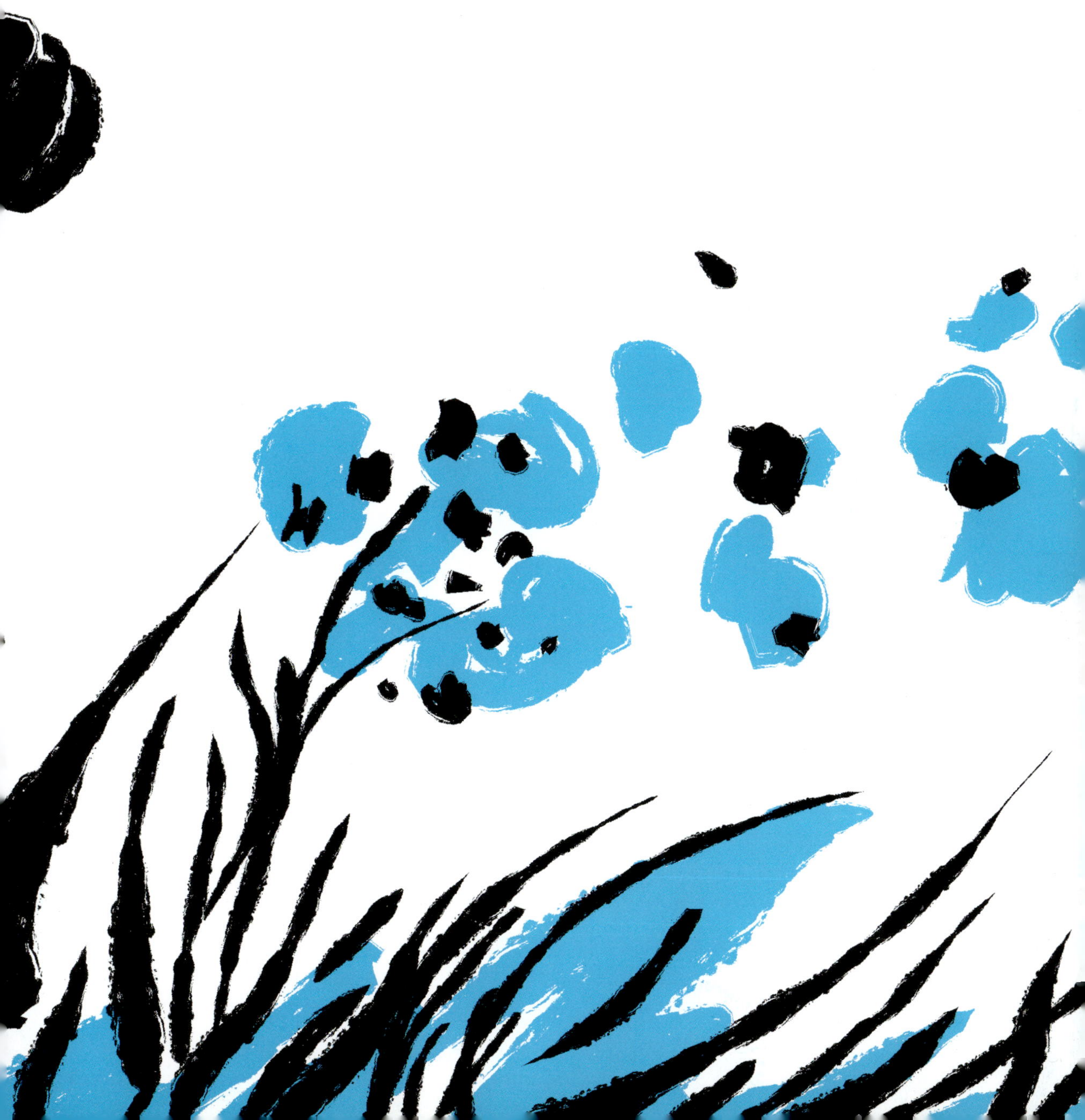

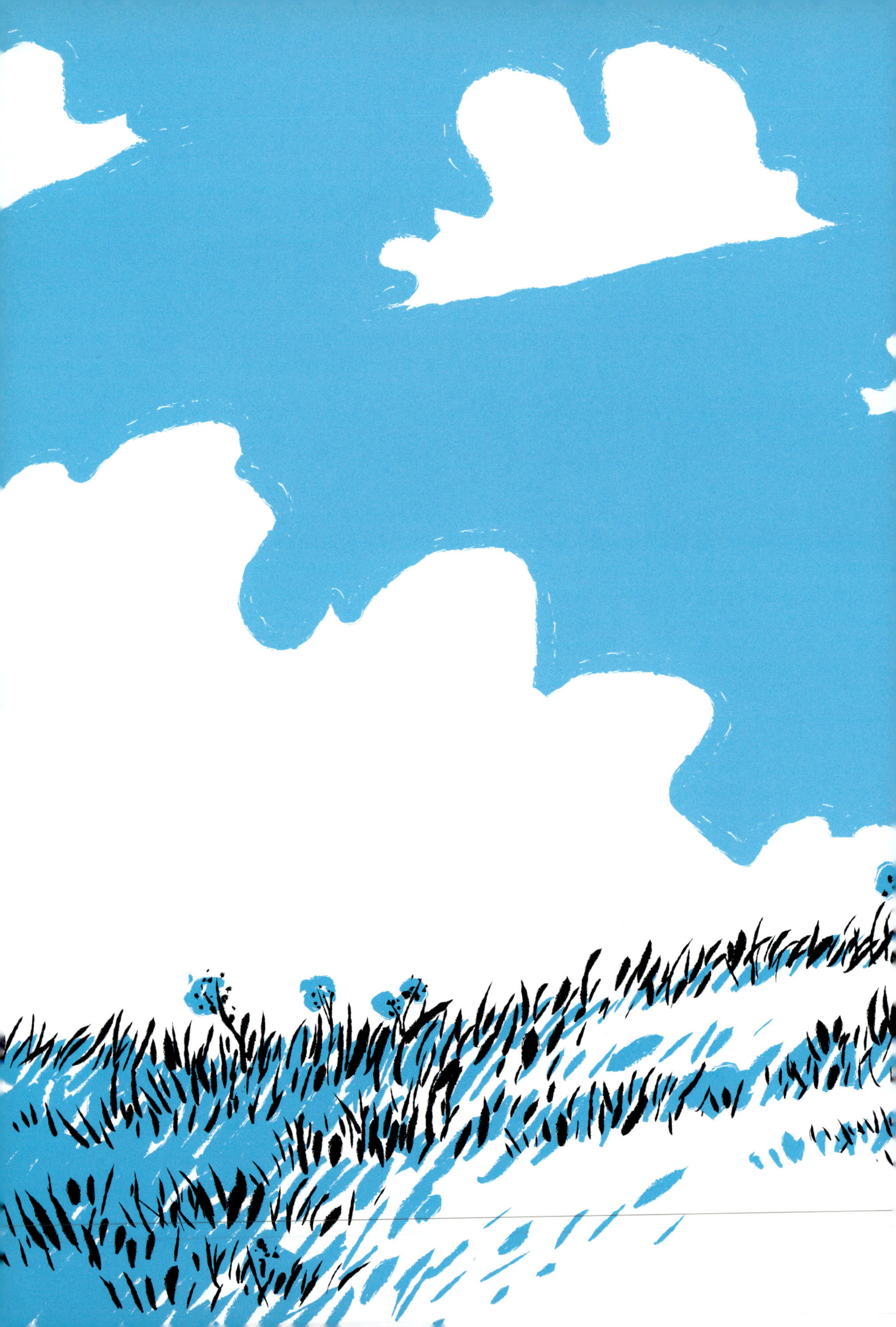

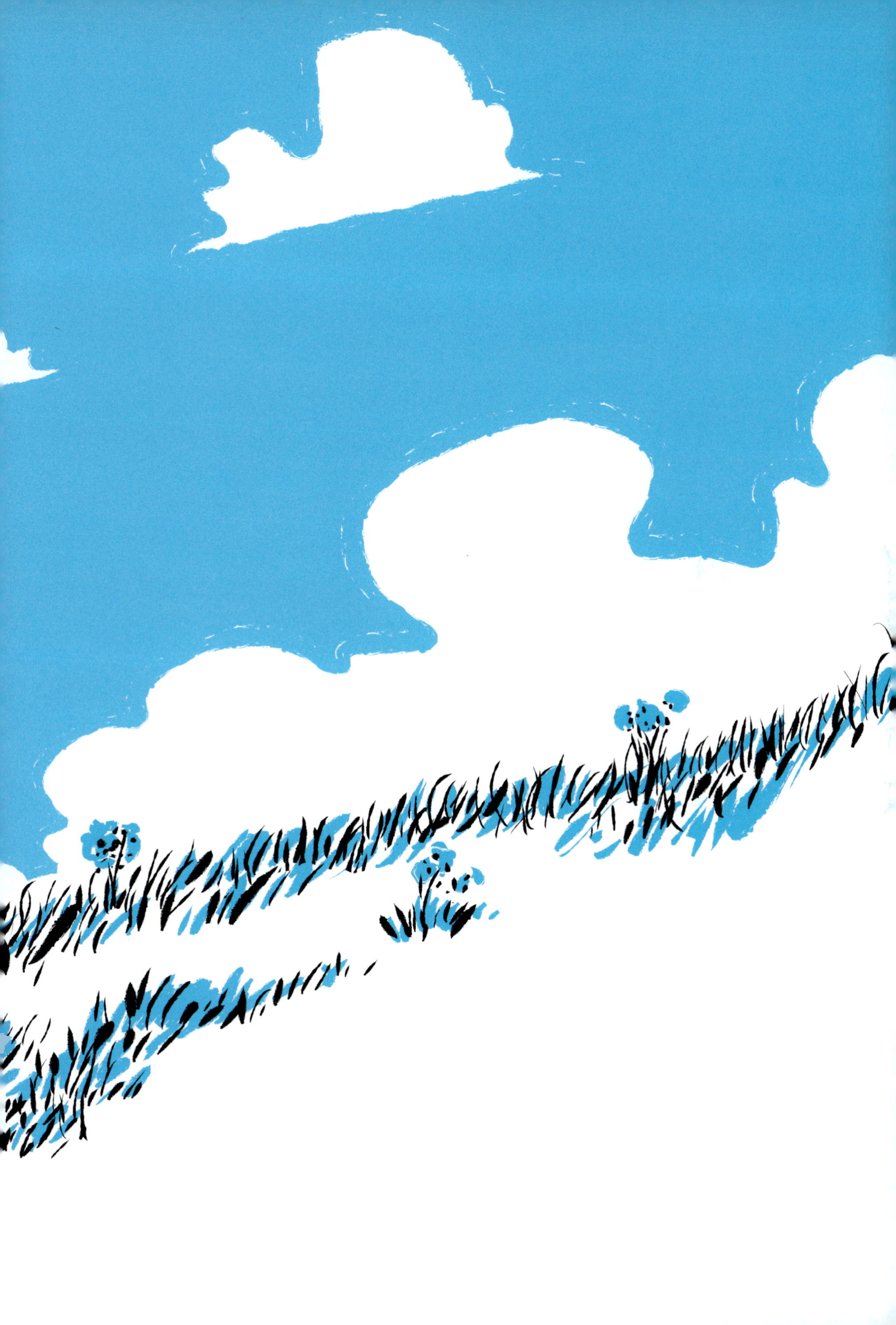

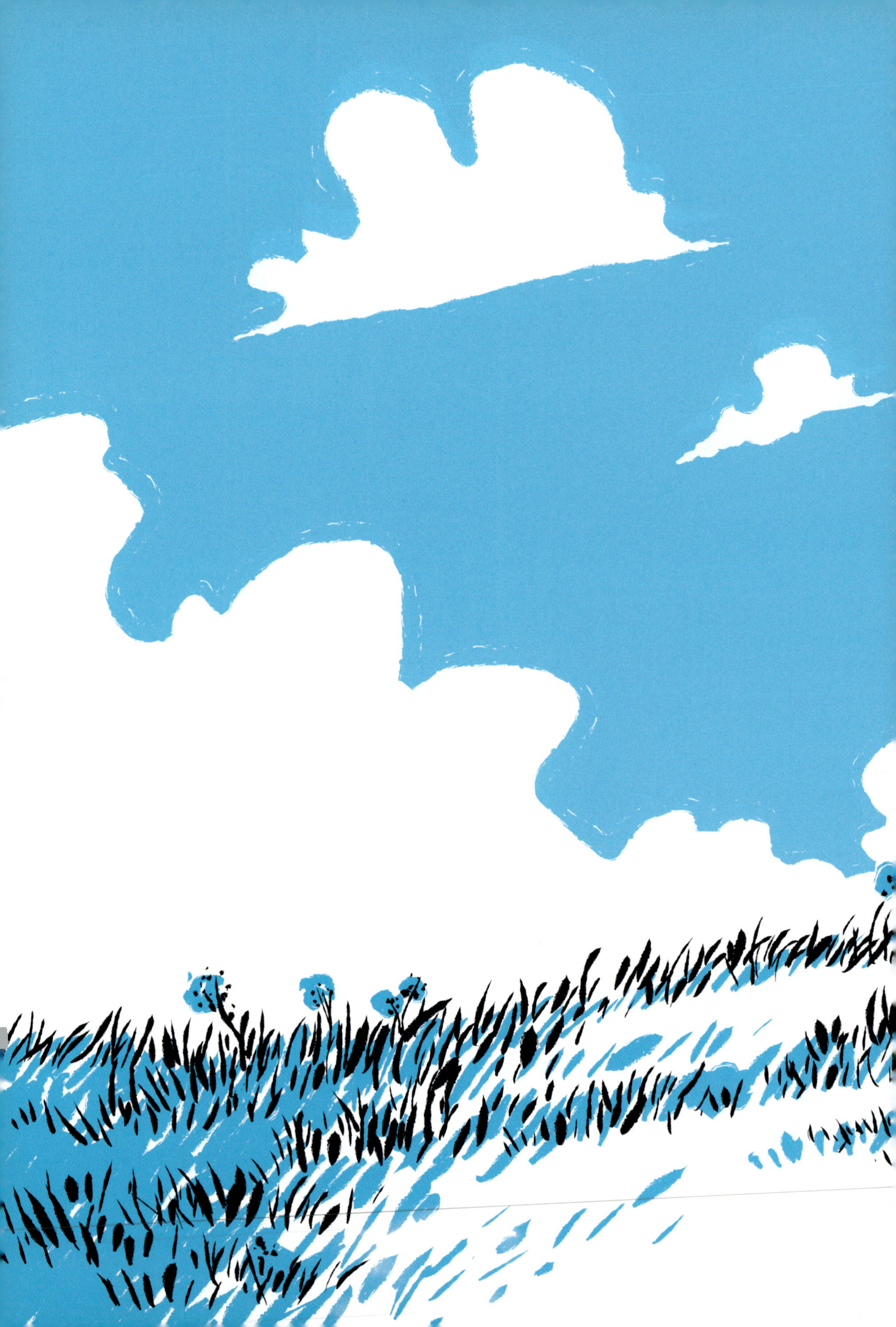

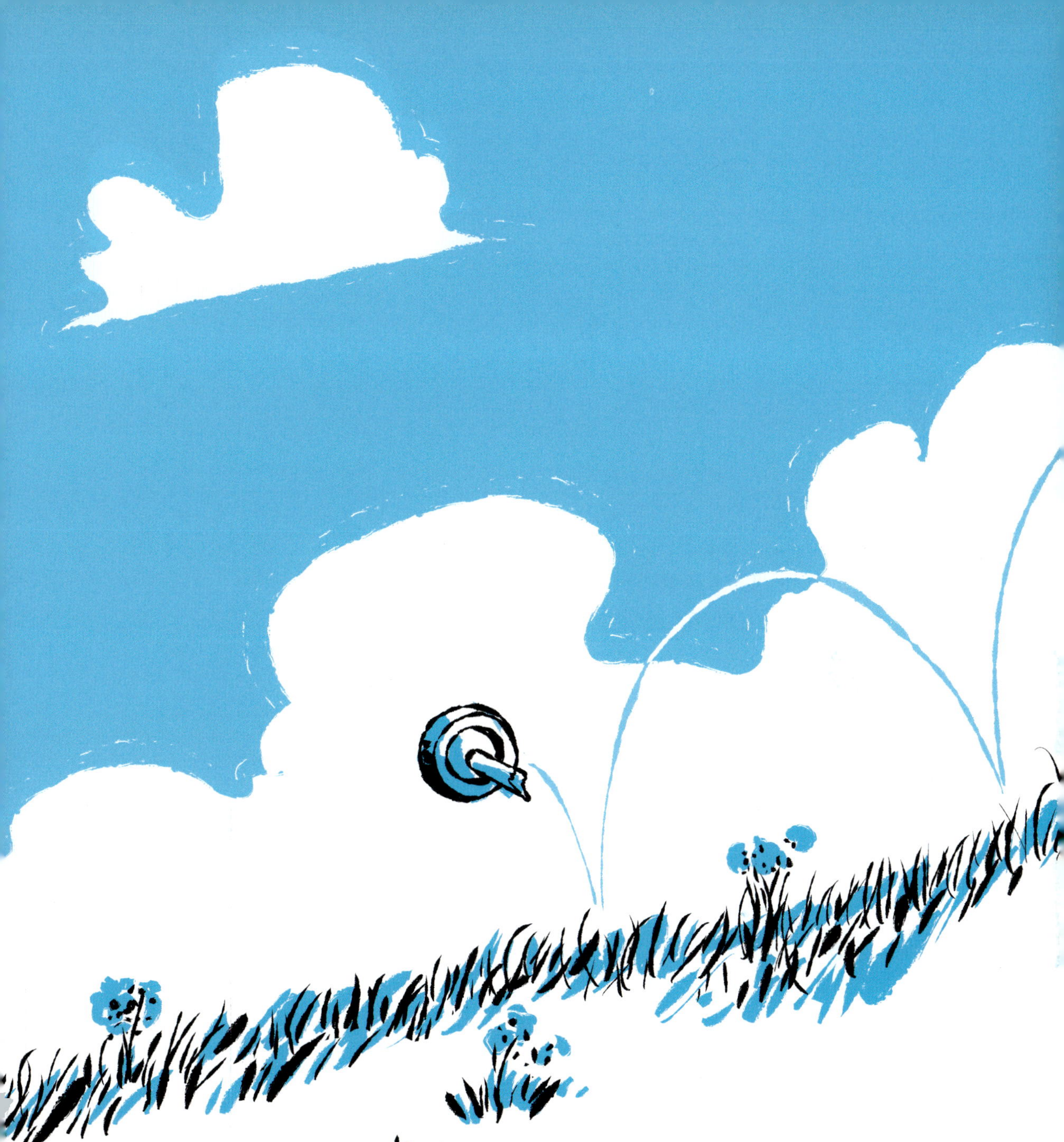

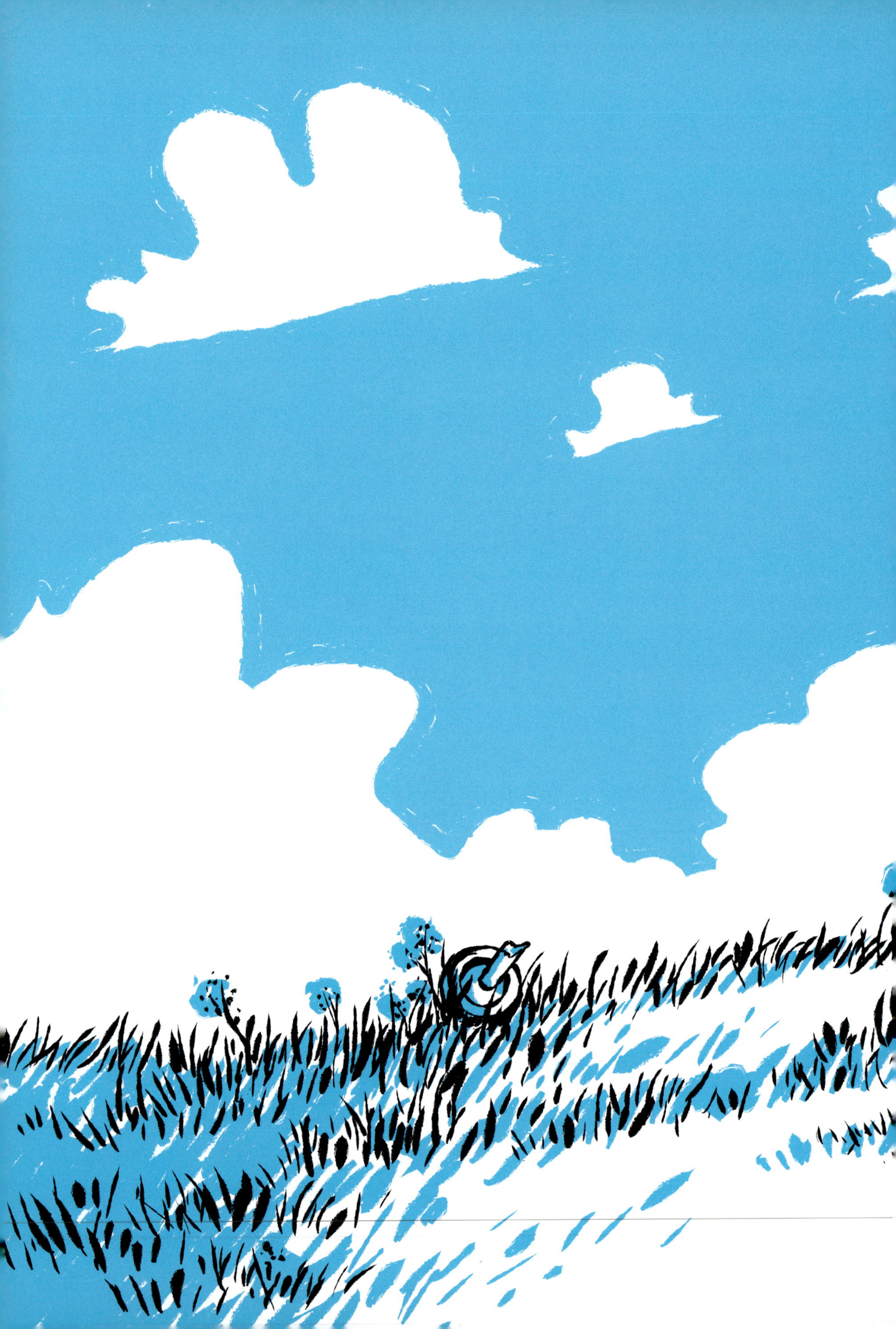

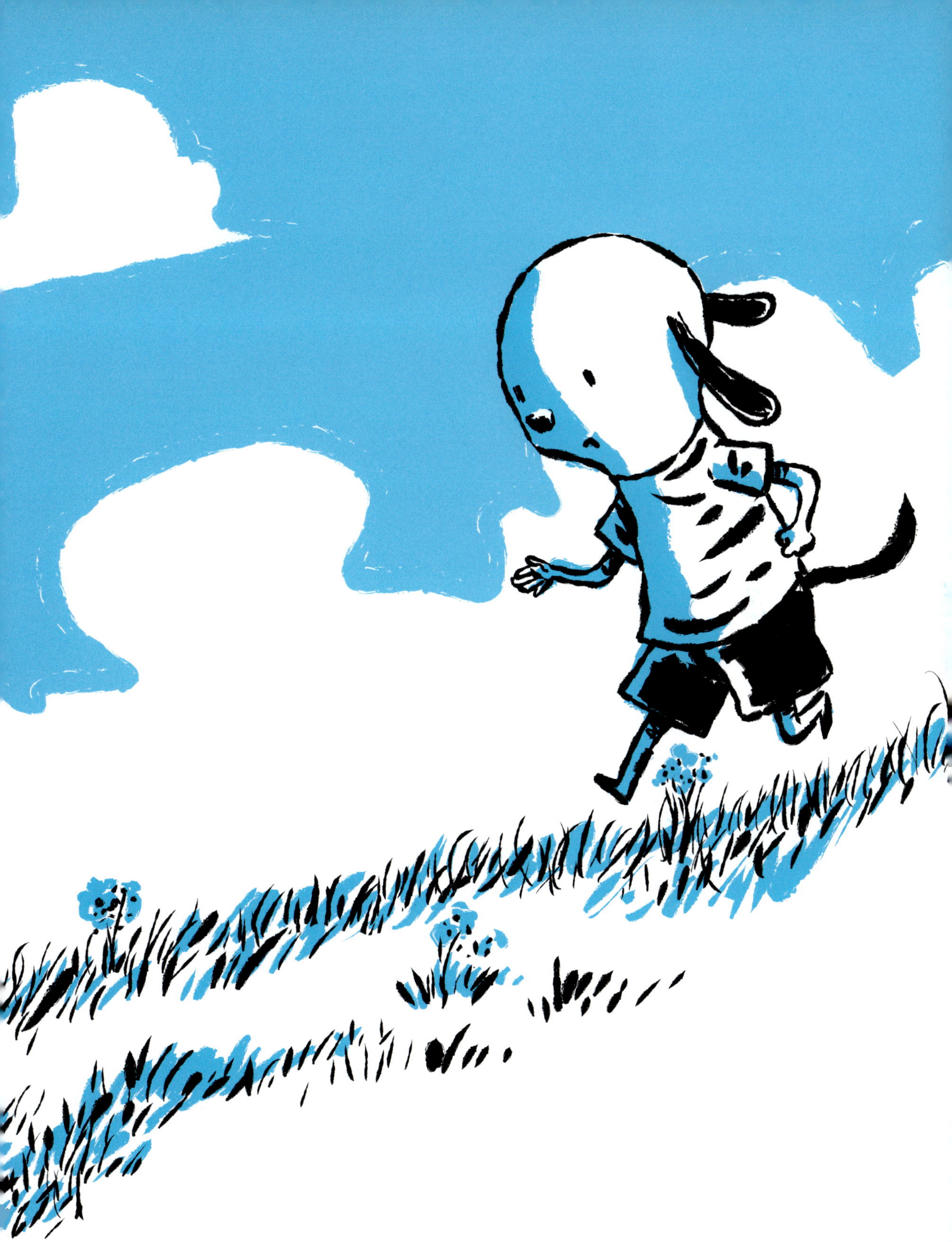

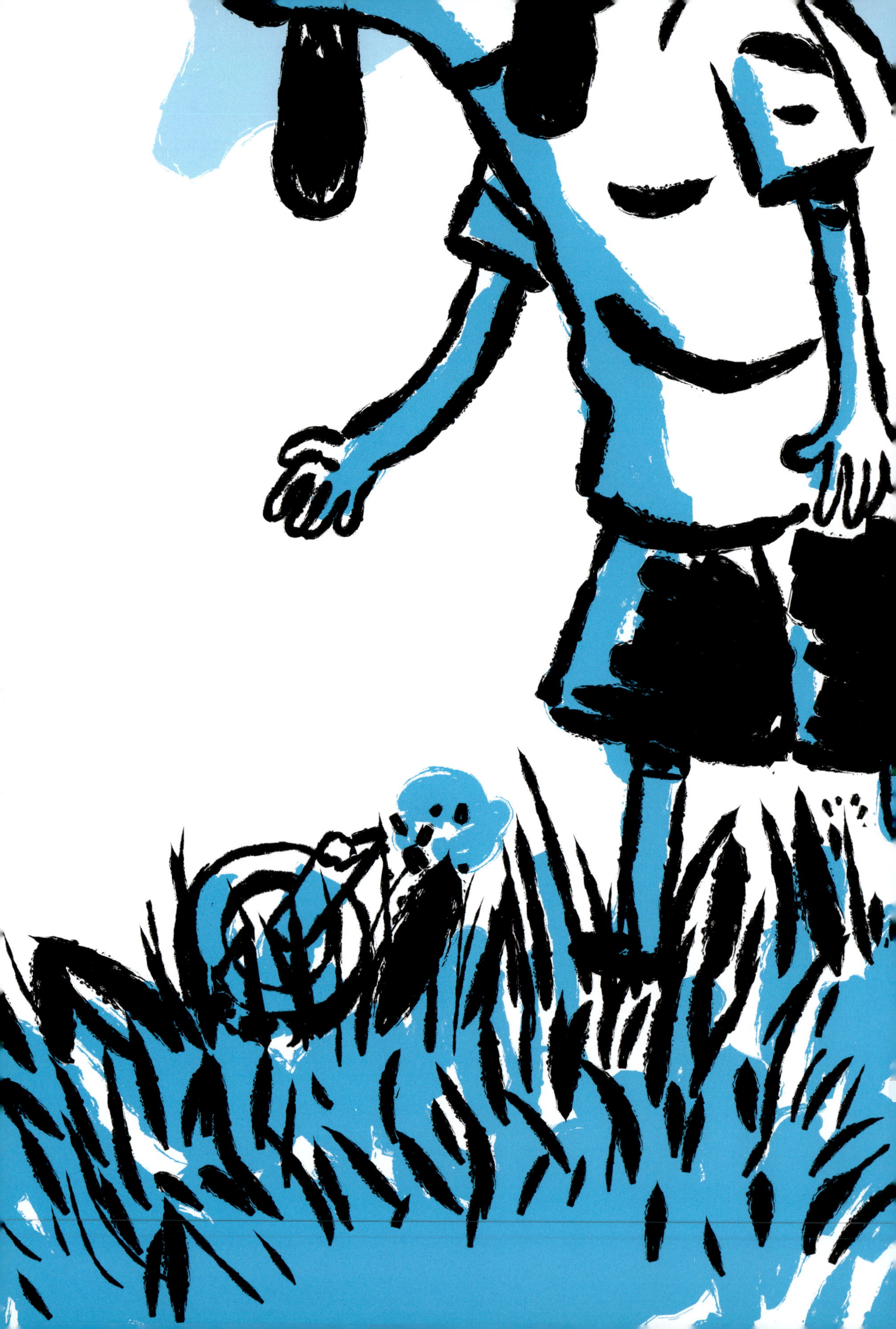

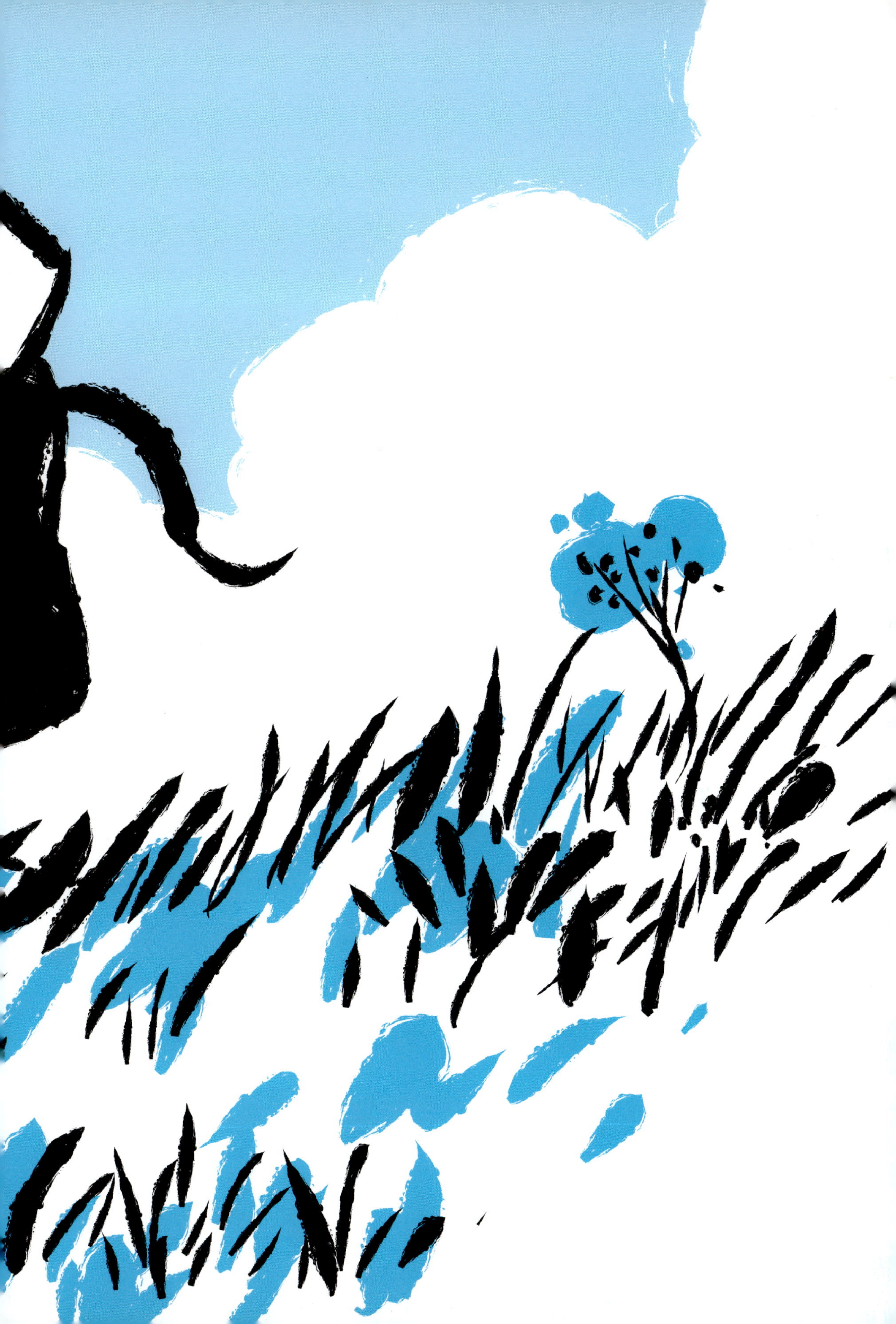

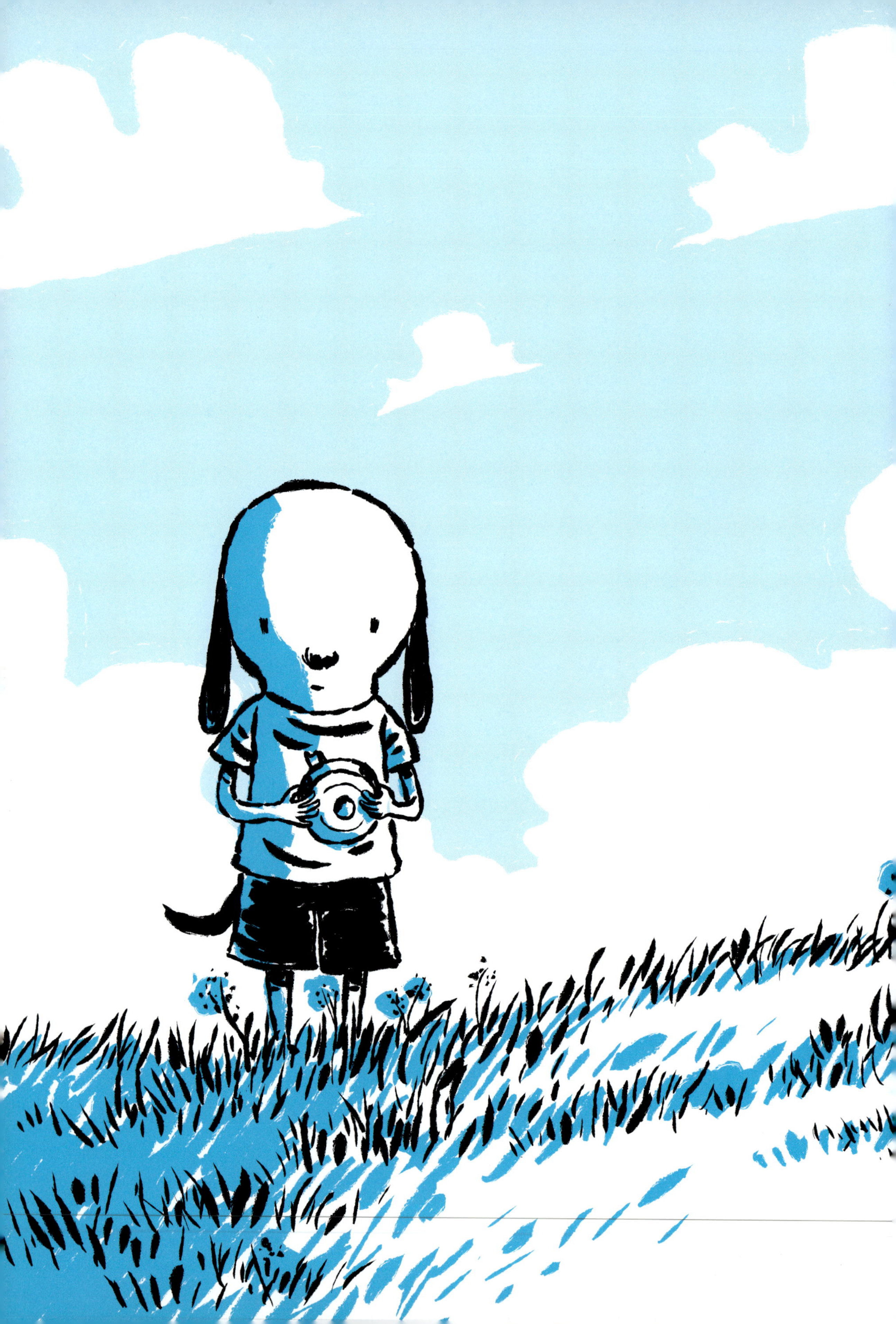

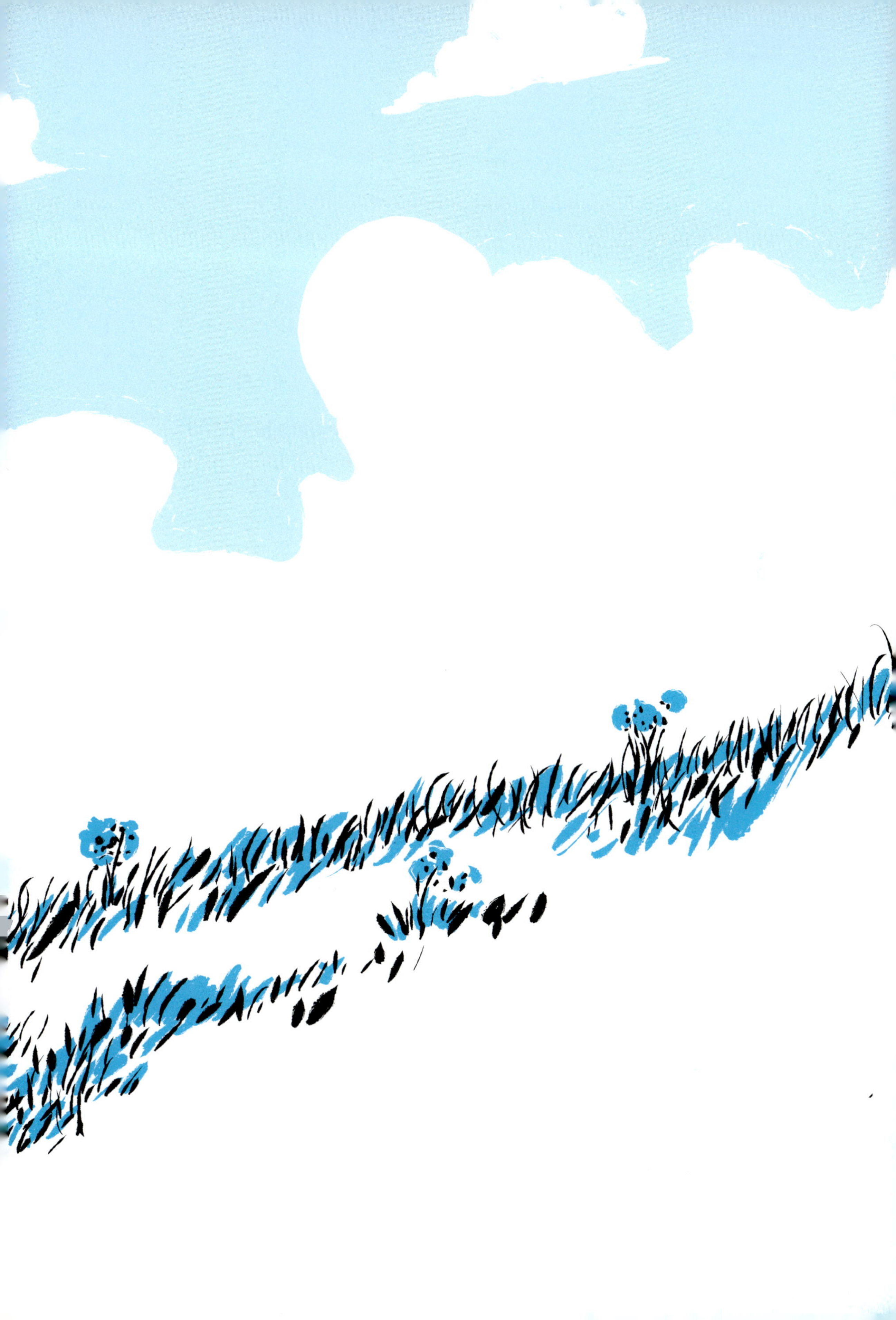

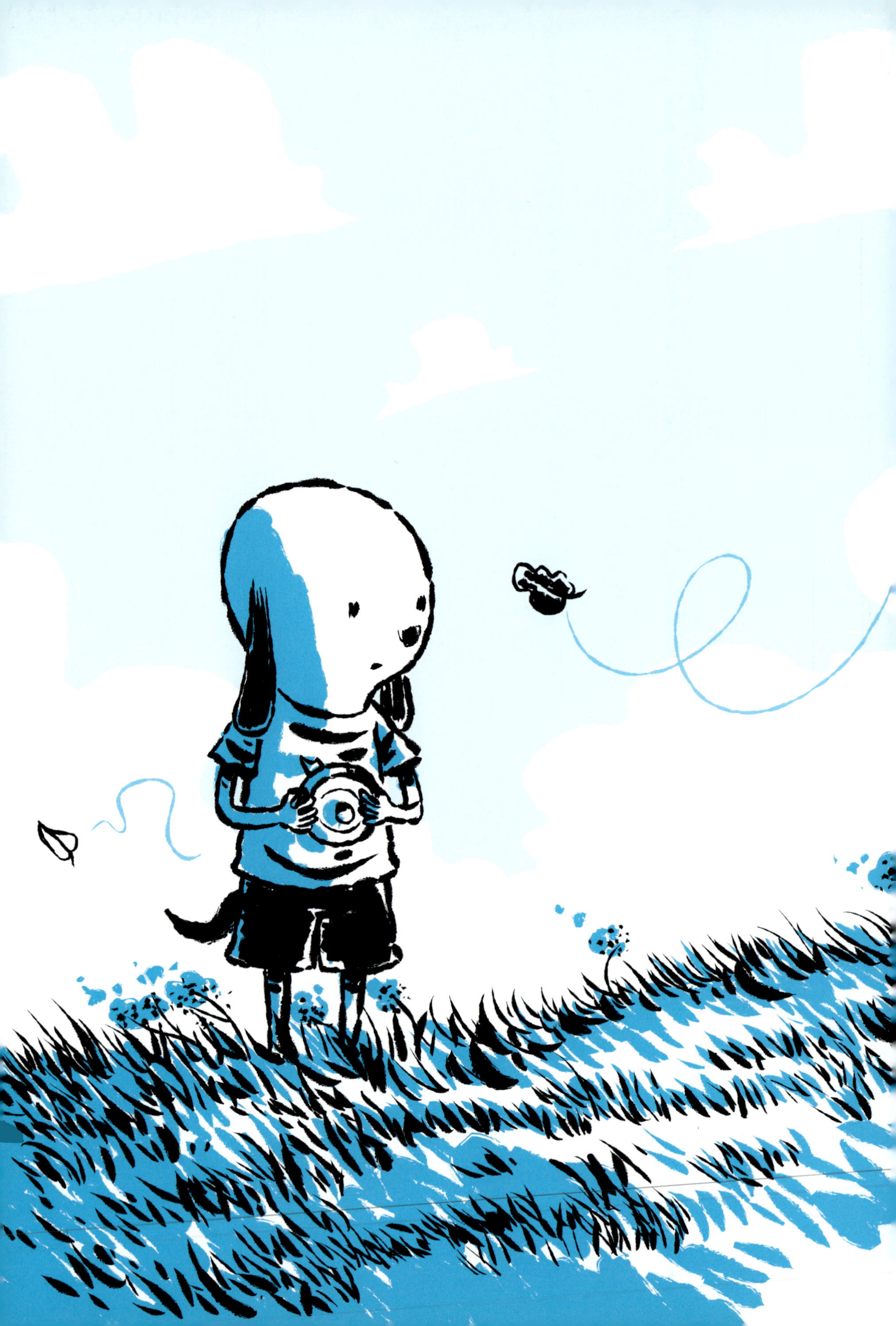

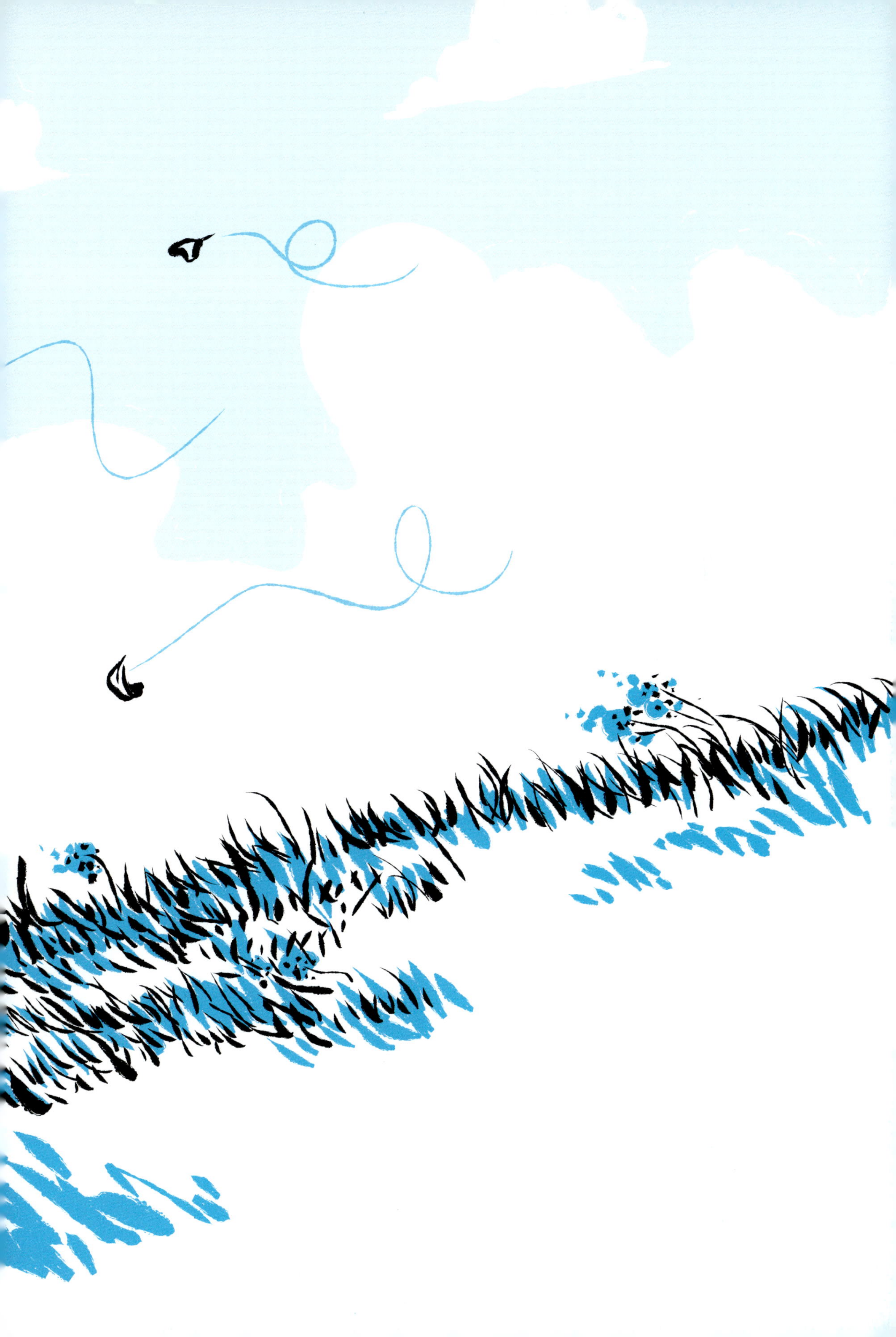

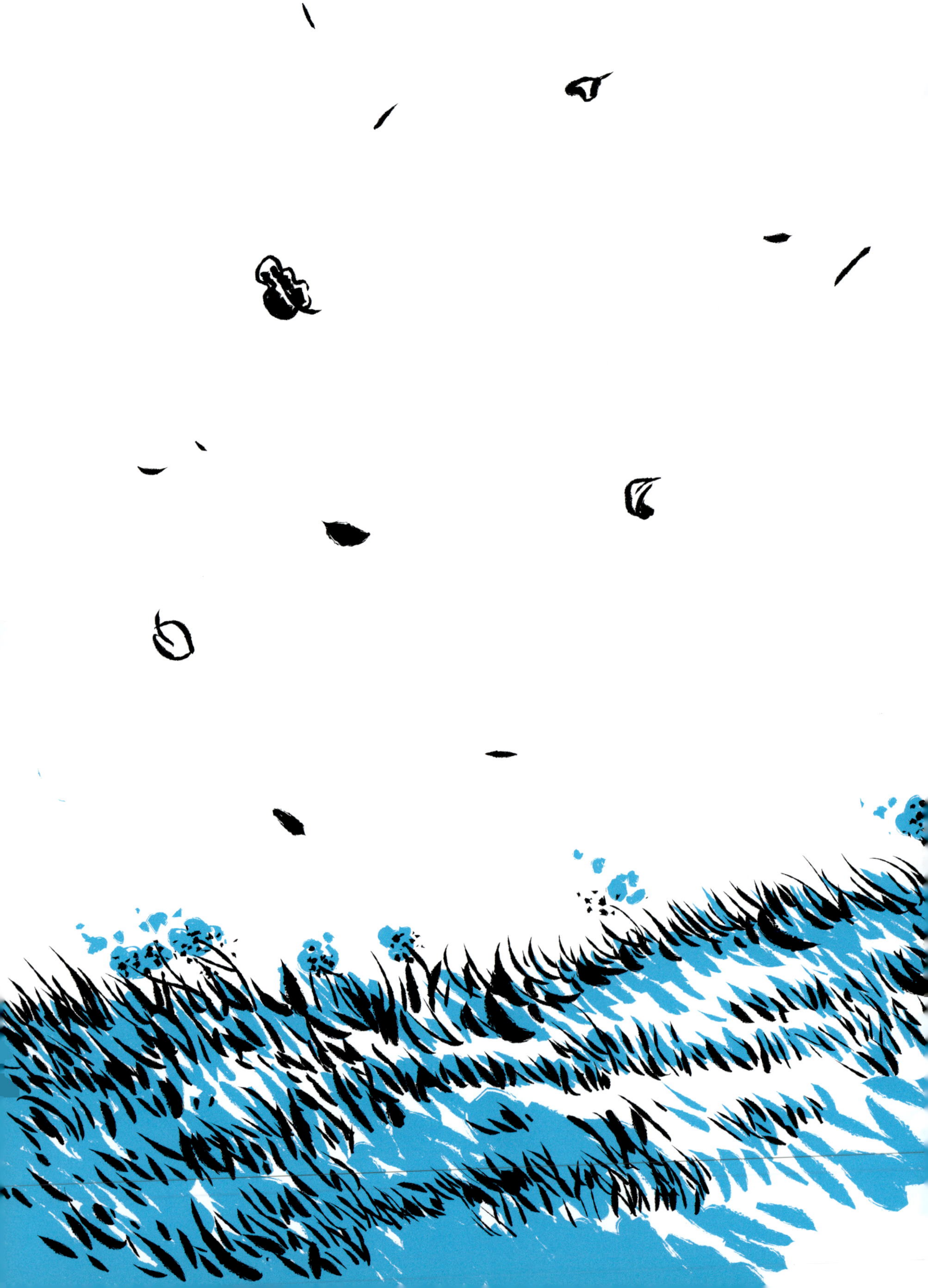

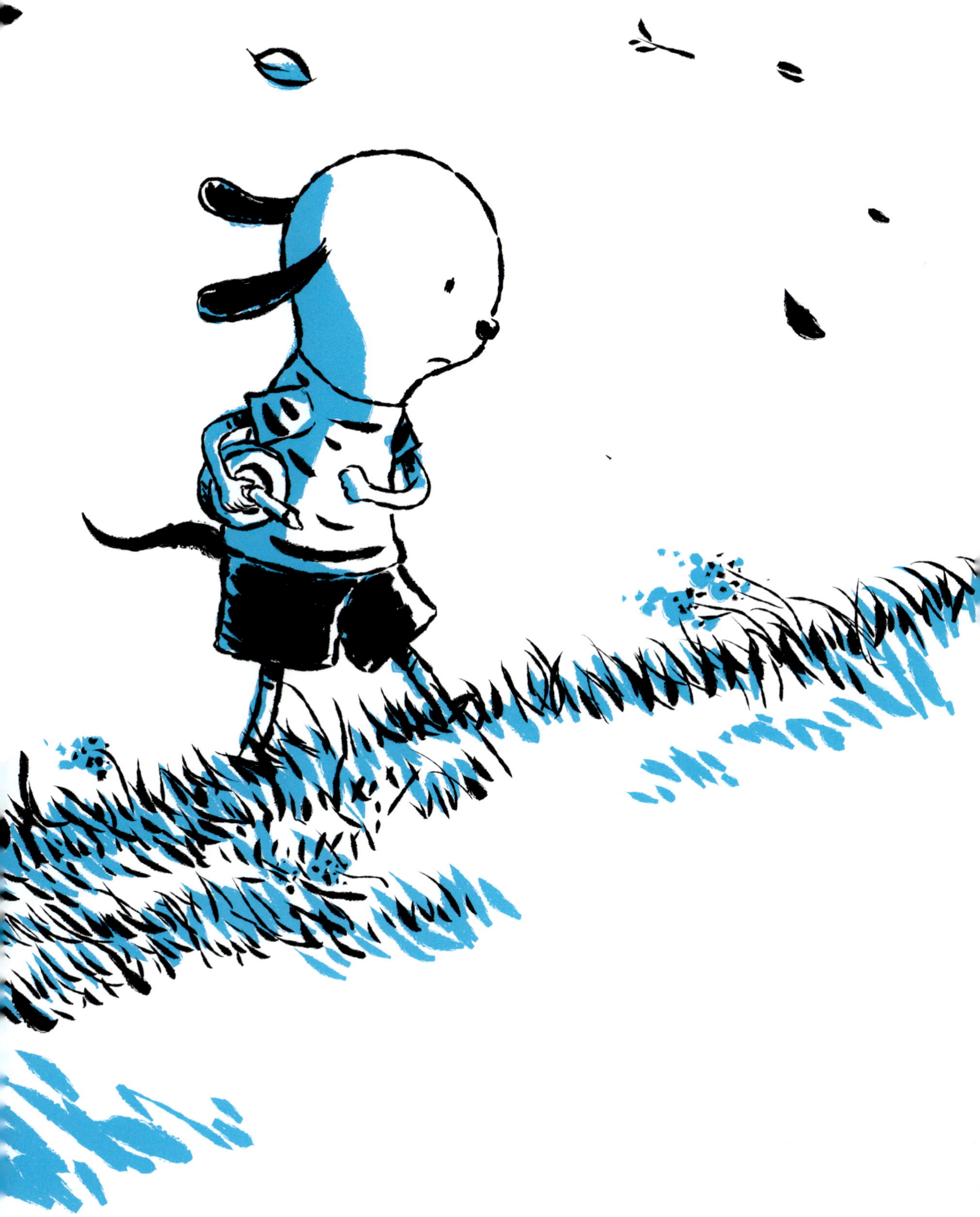

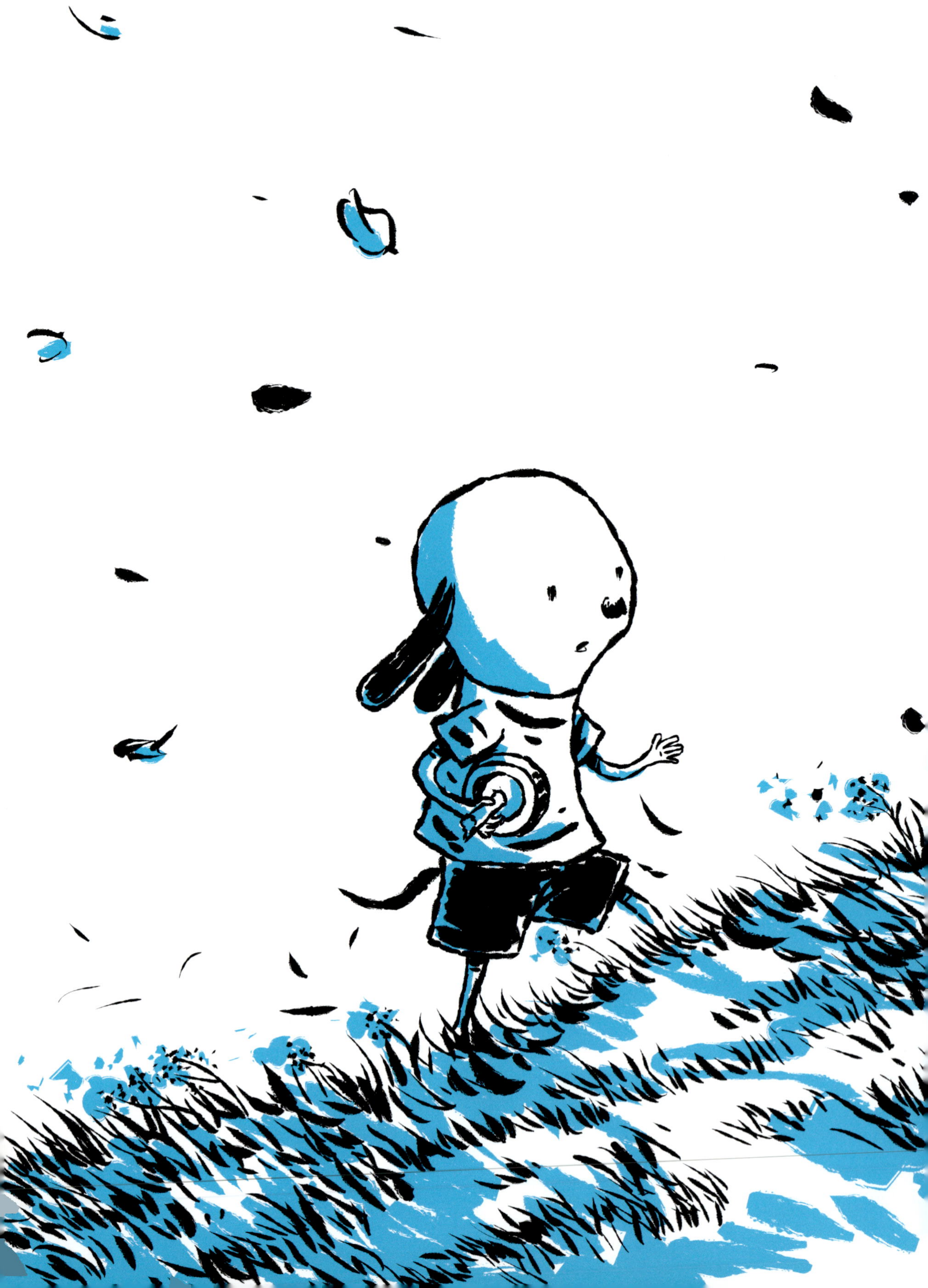

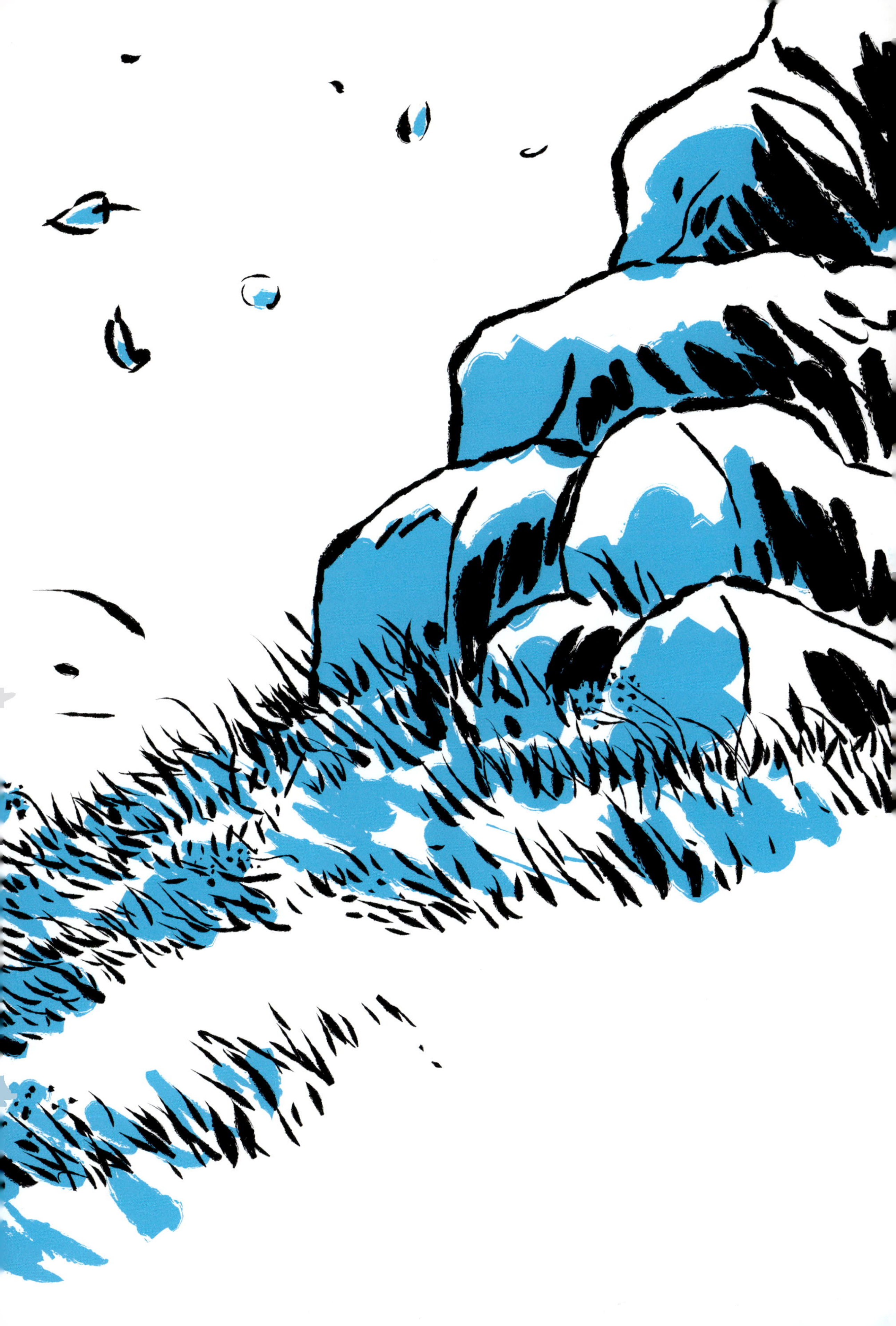

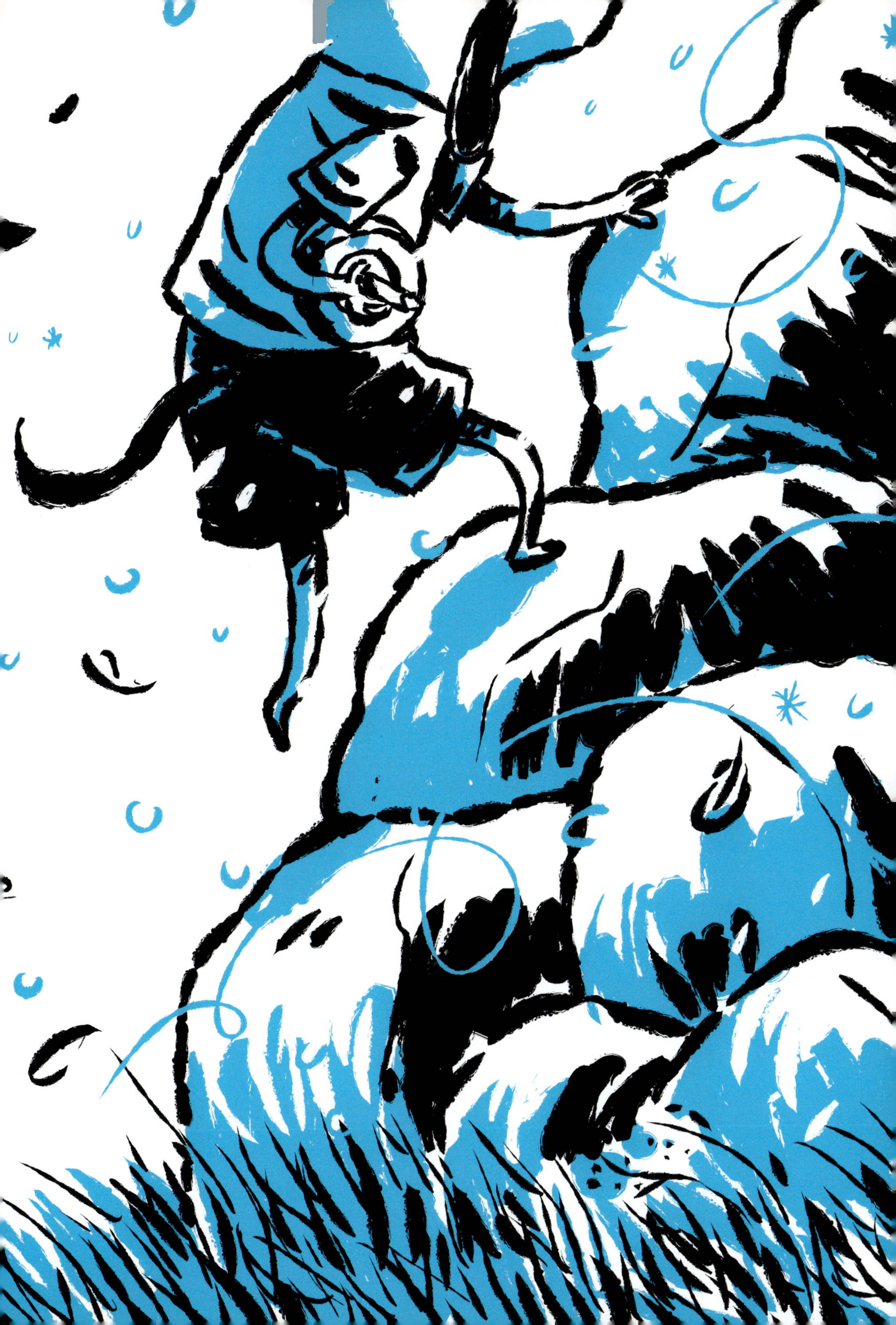

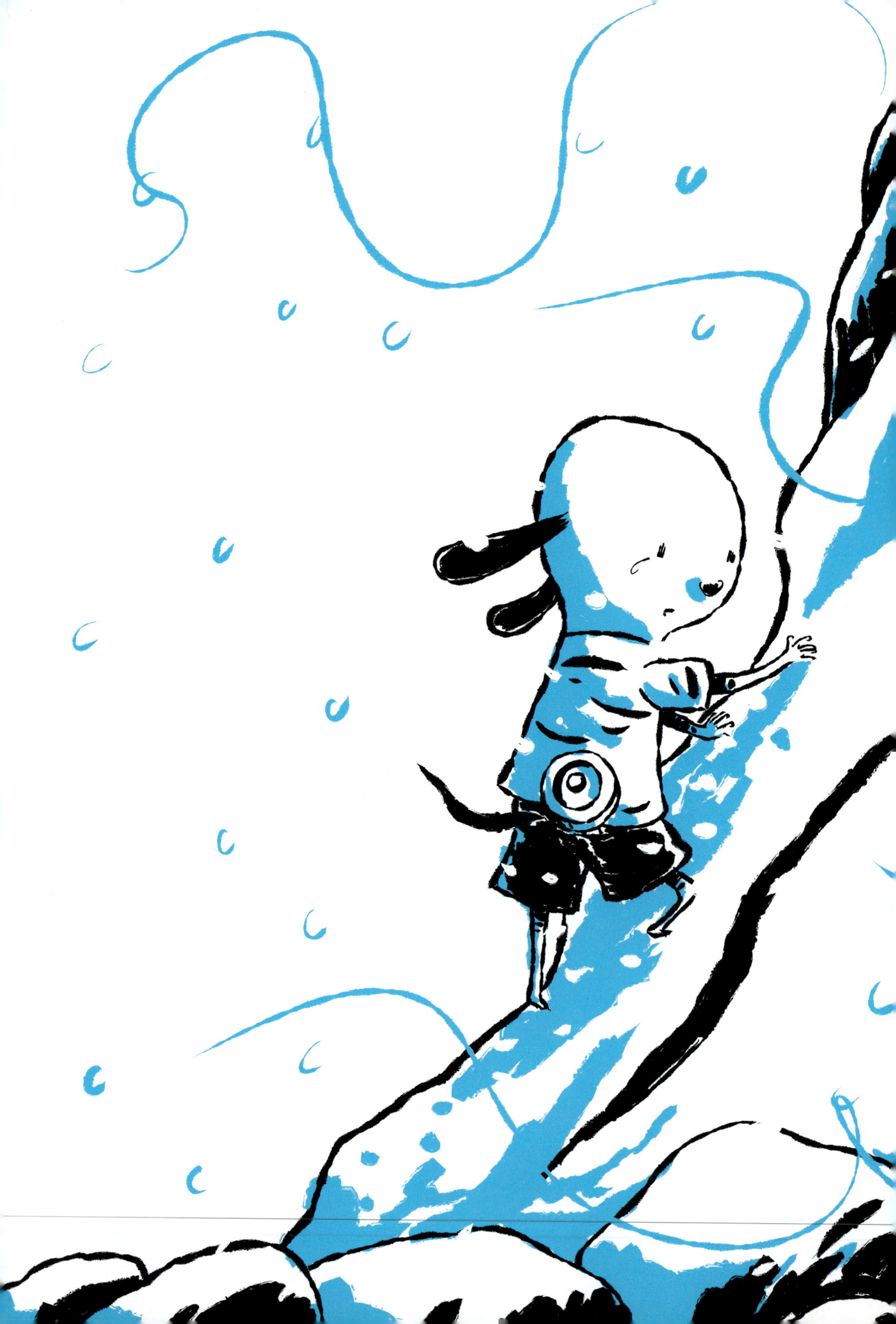

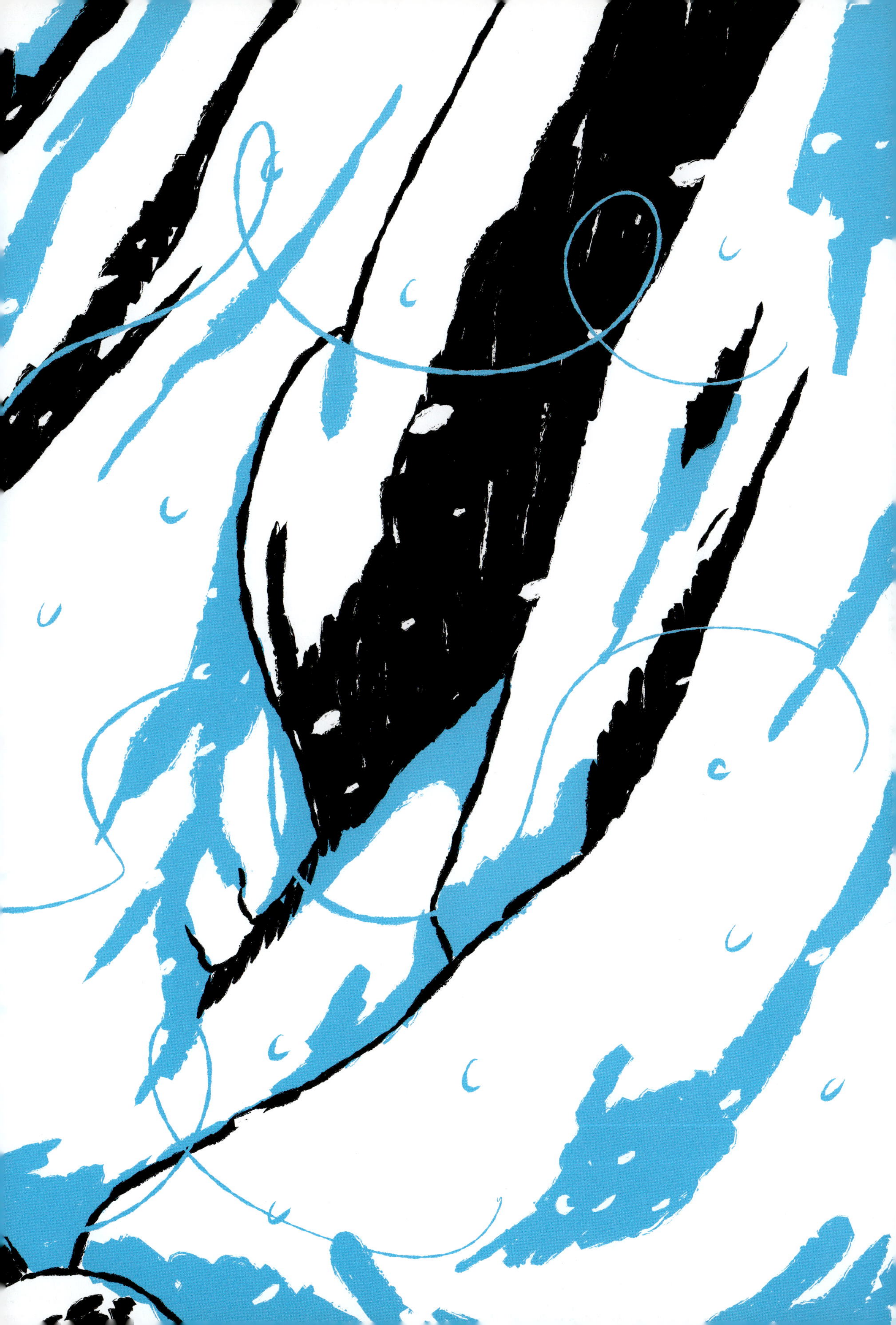

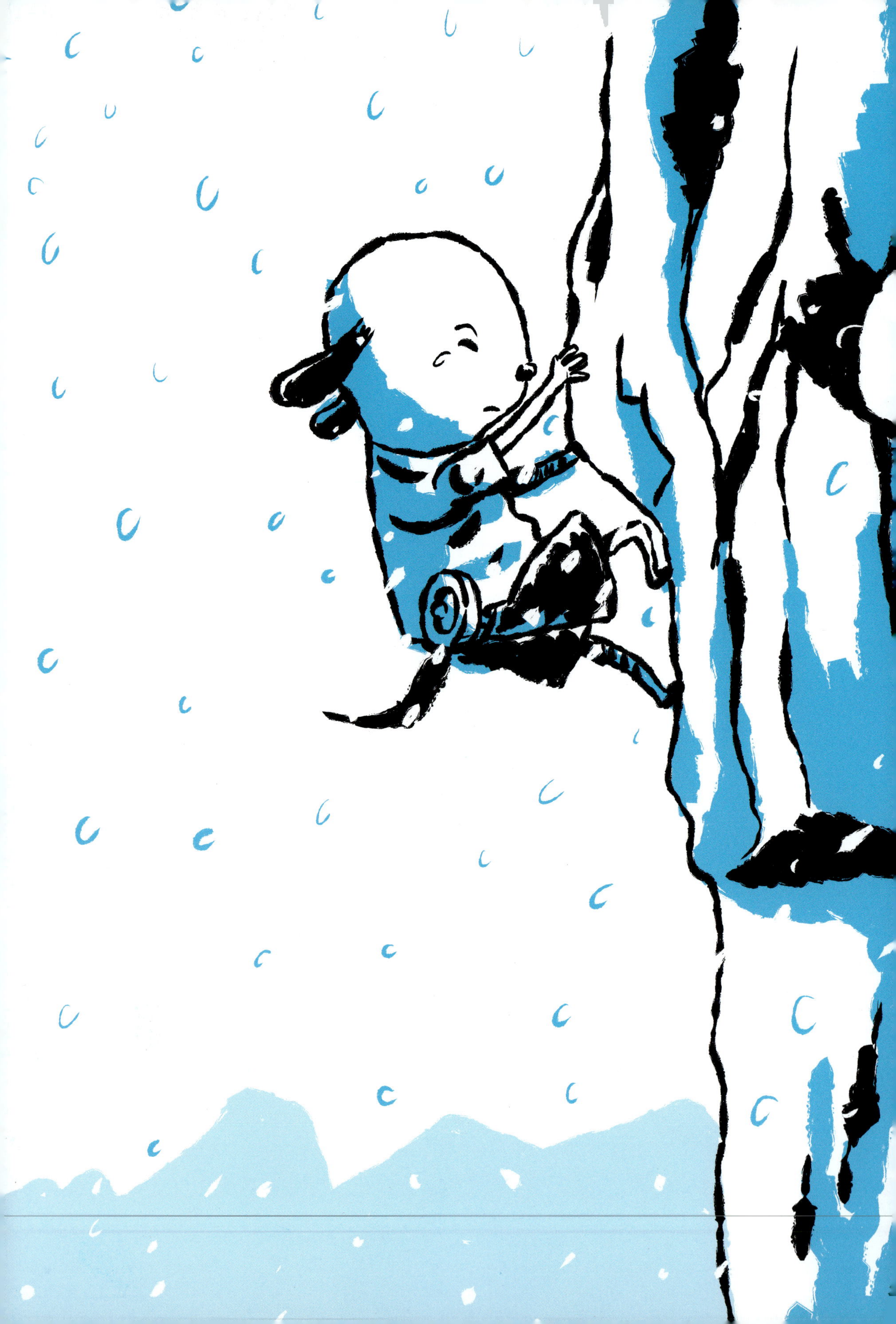

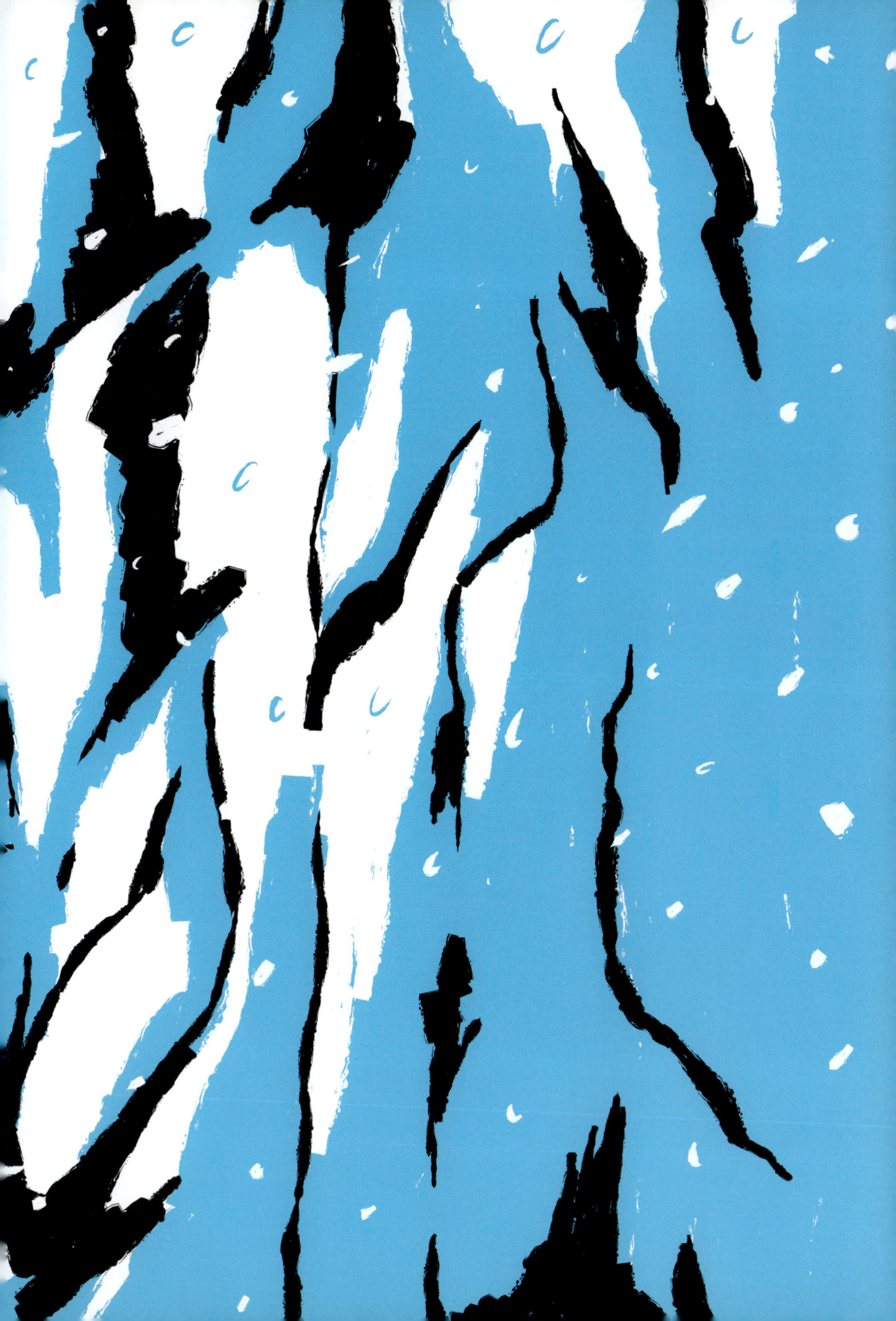

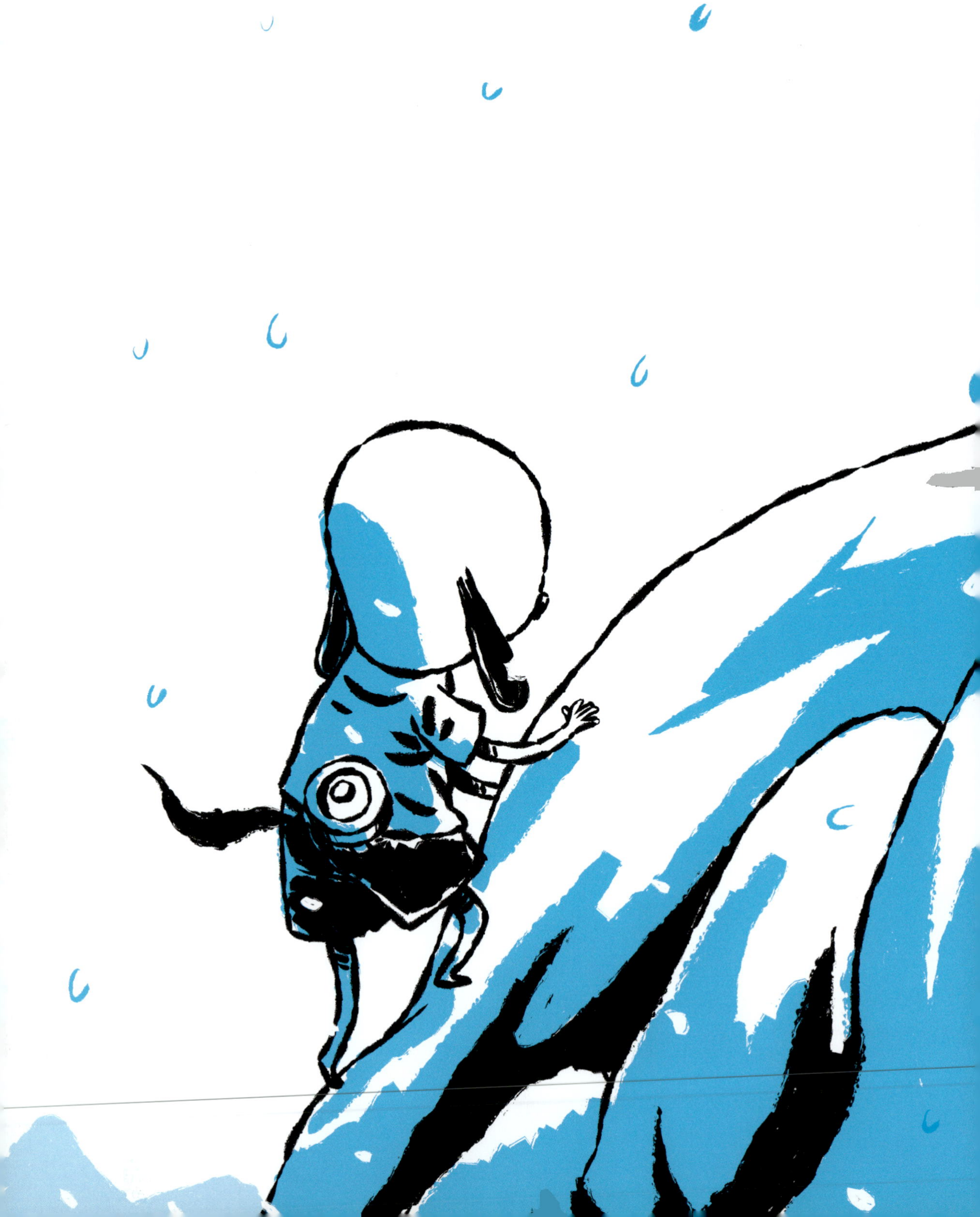

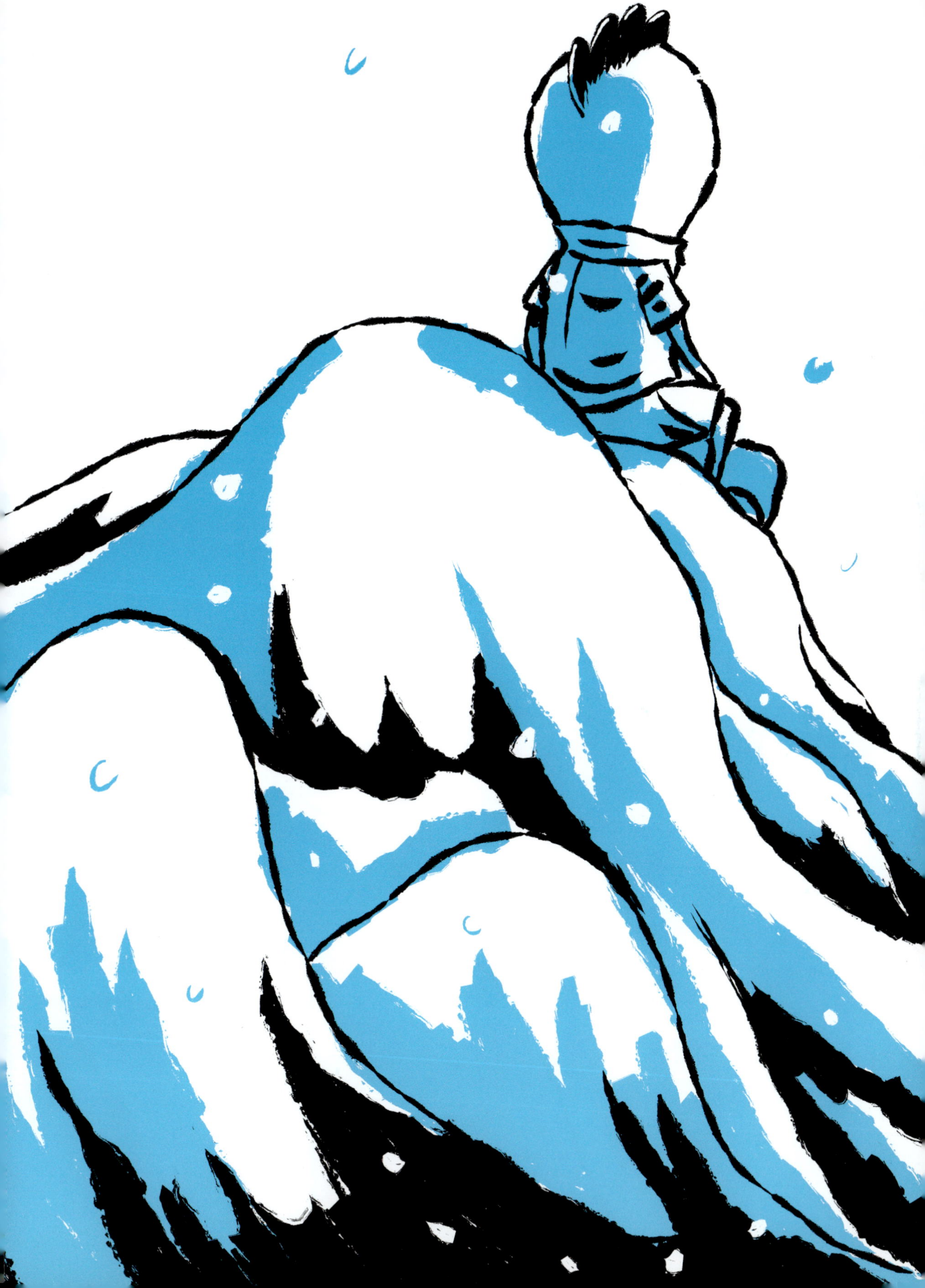

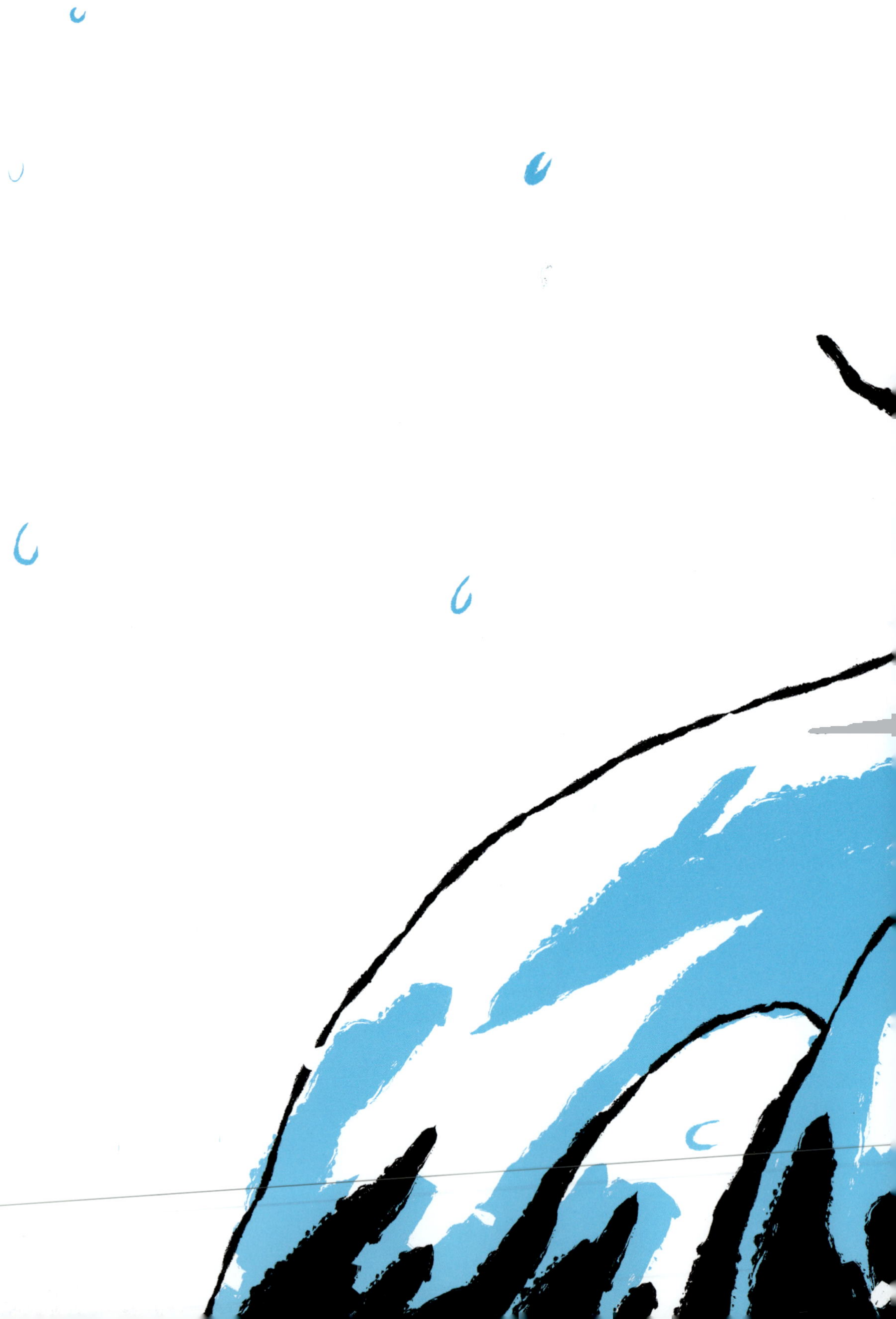

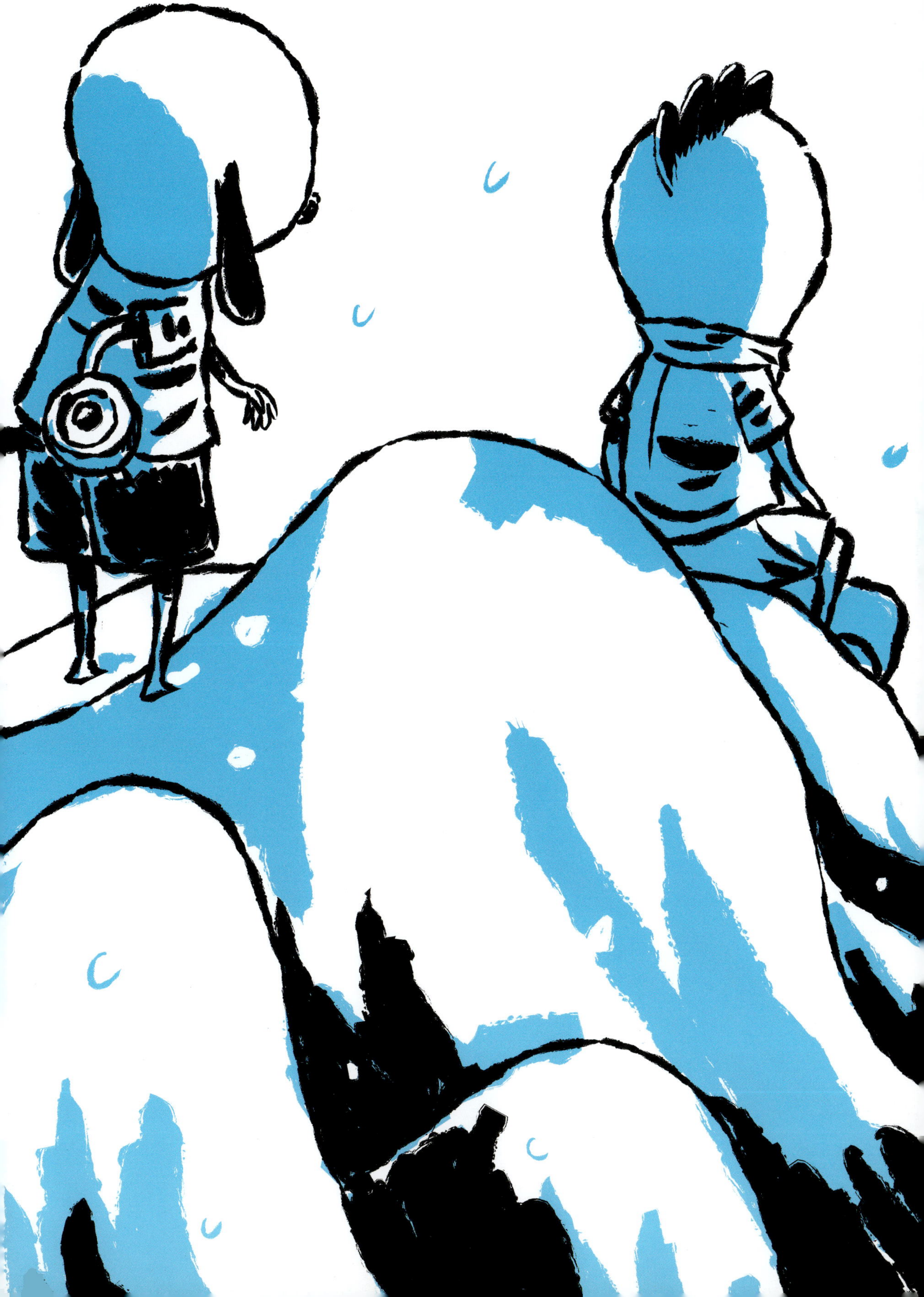

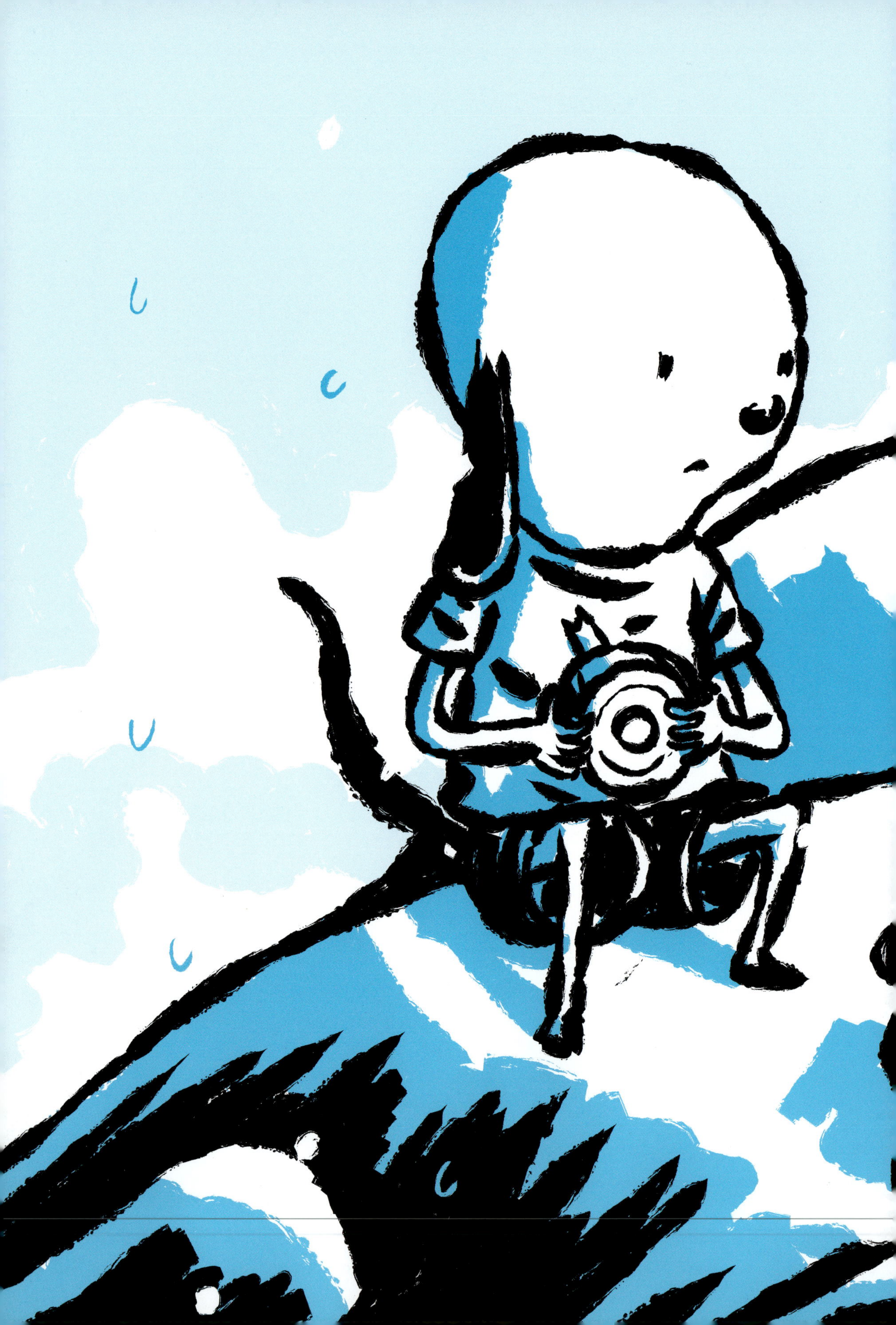

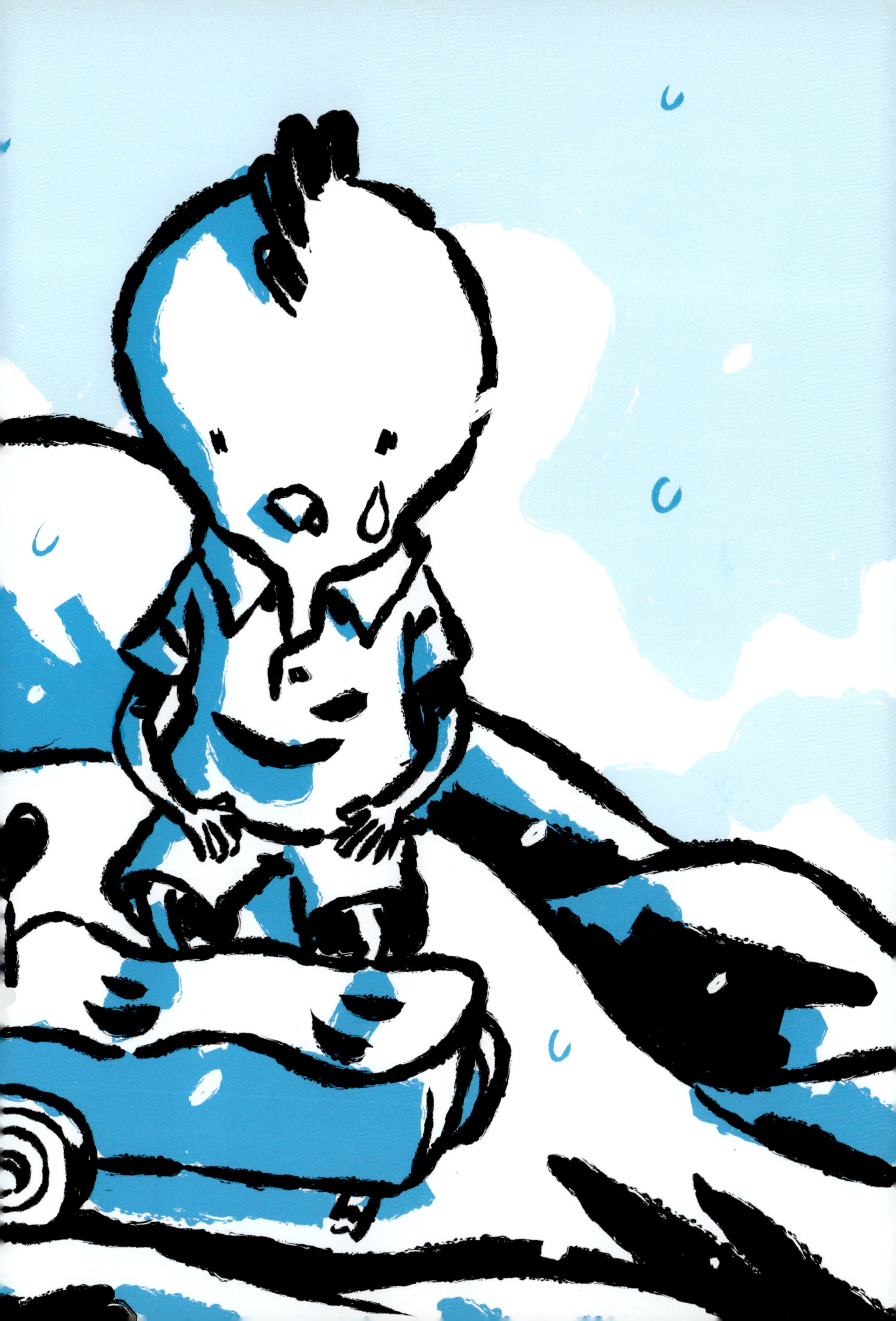

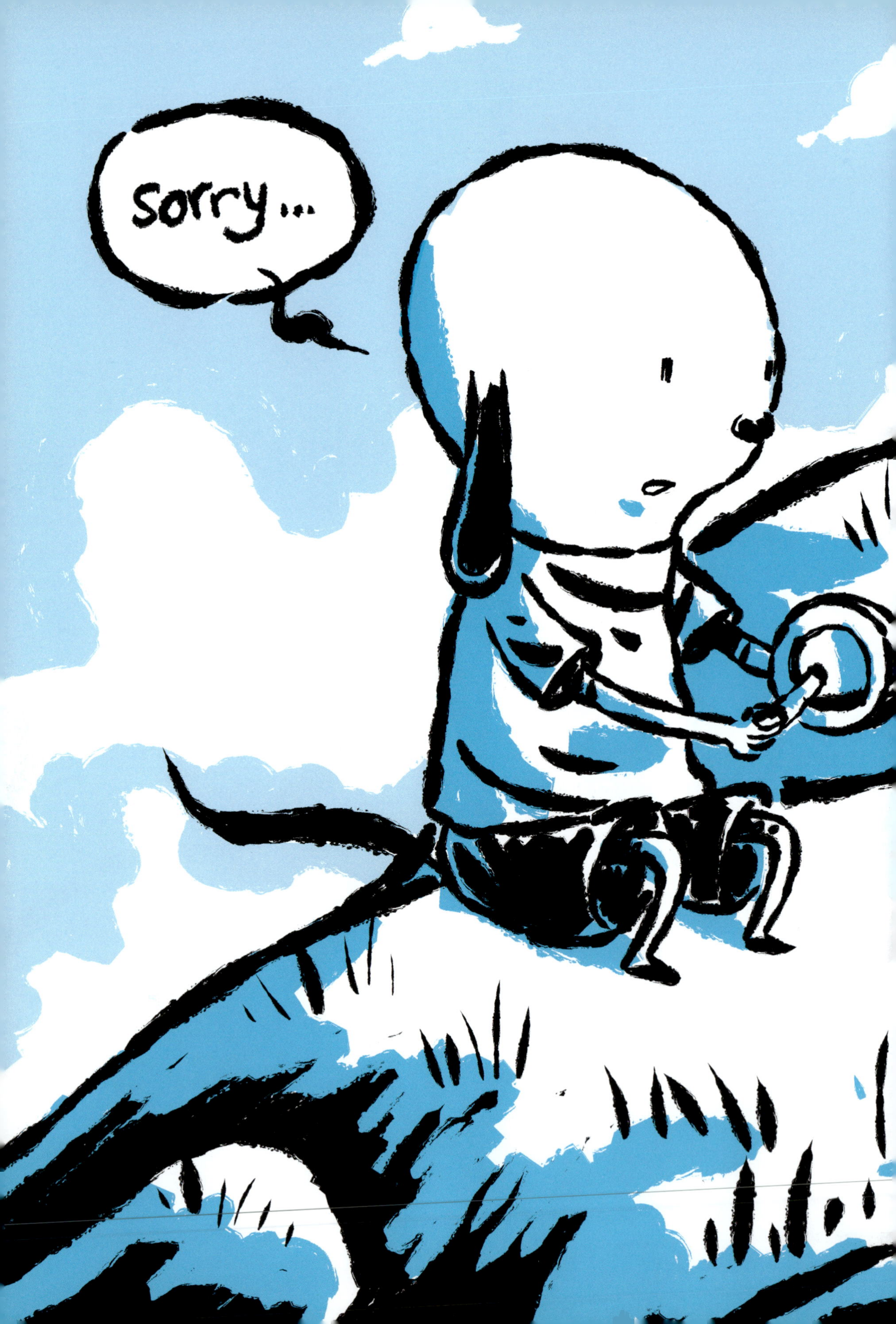
sorry...

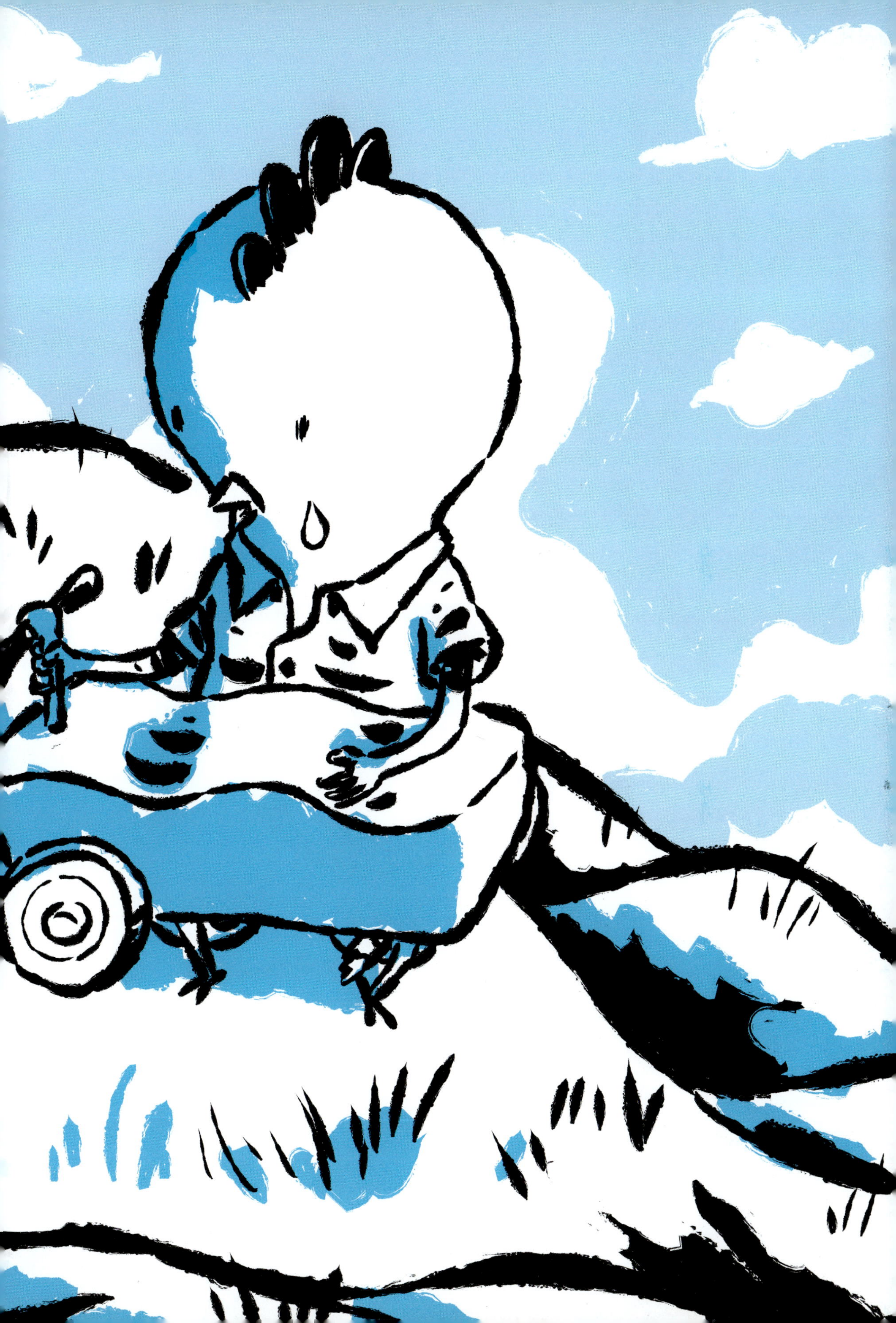

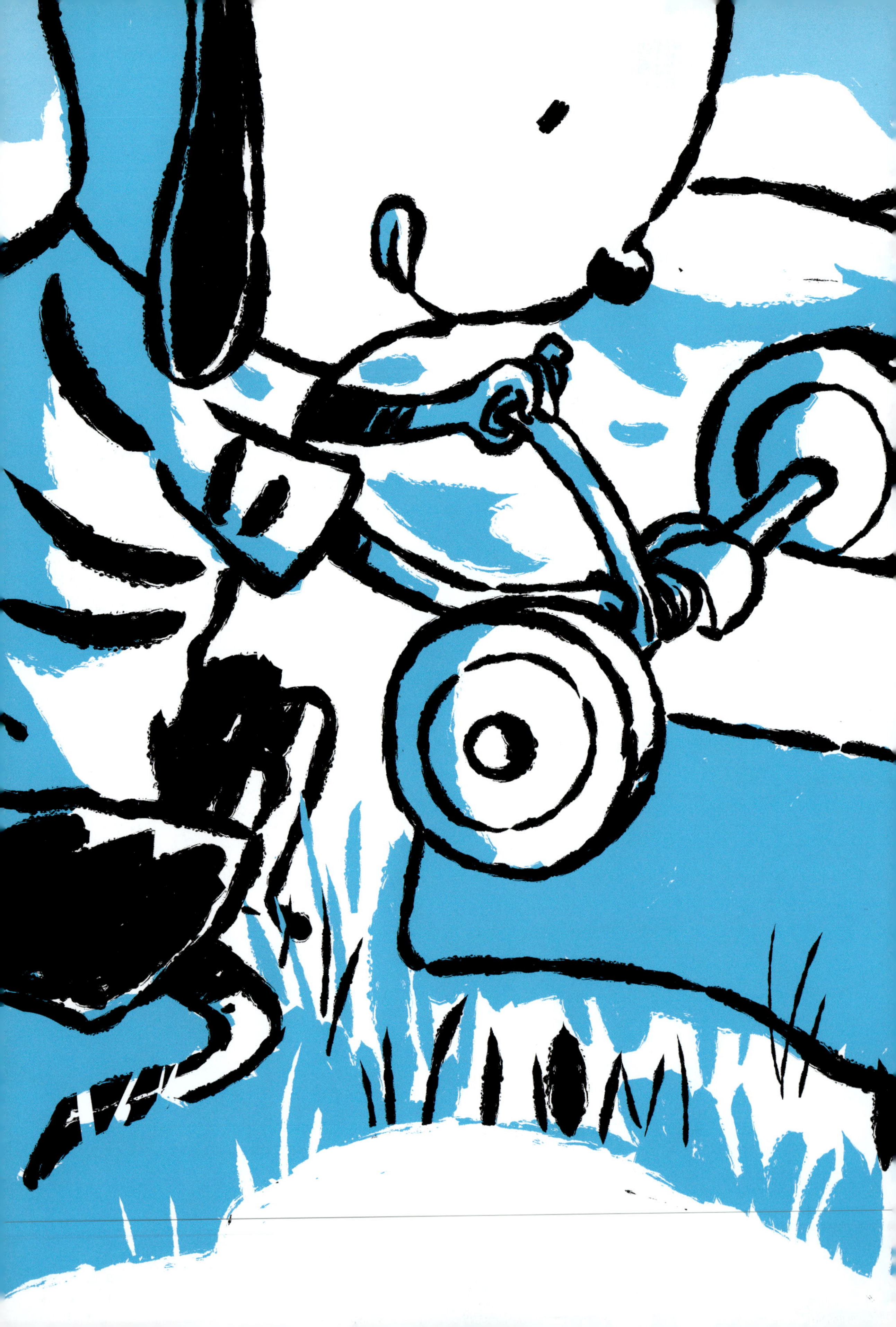

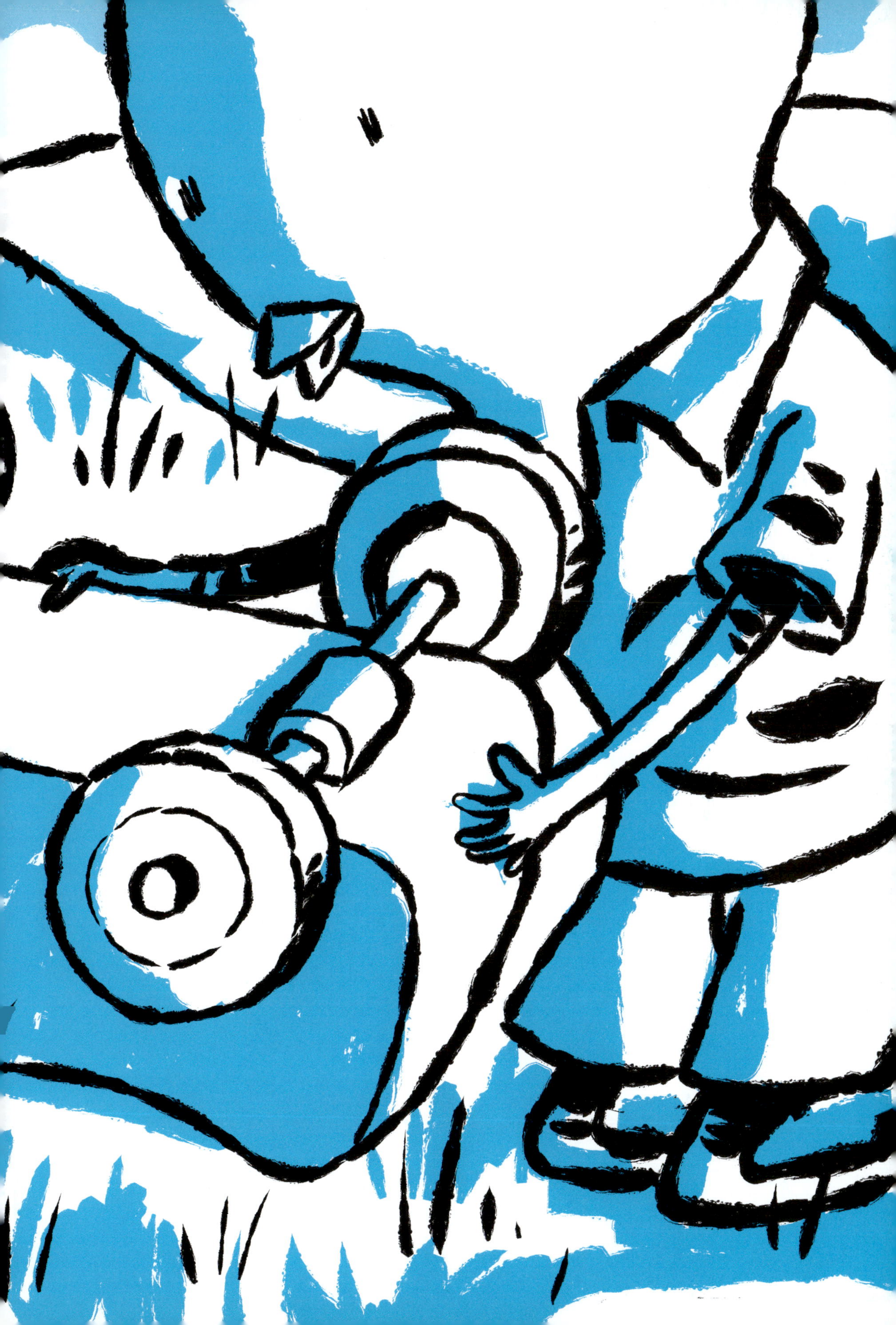

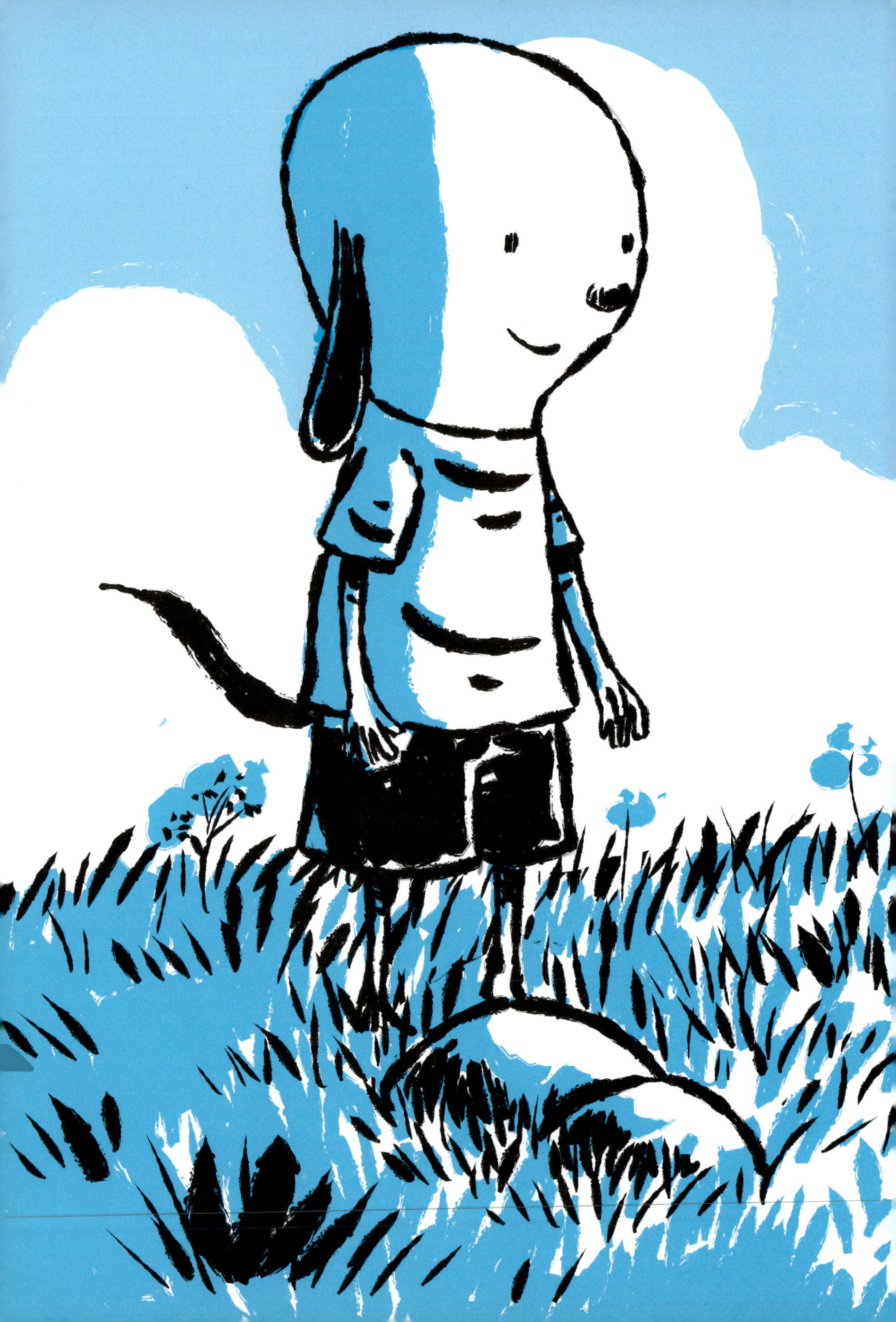

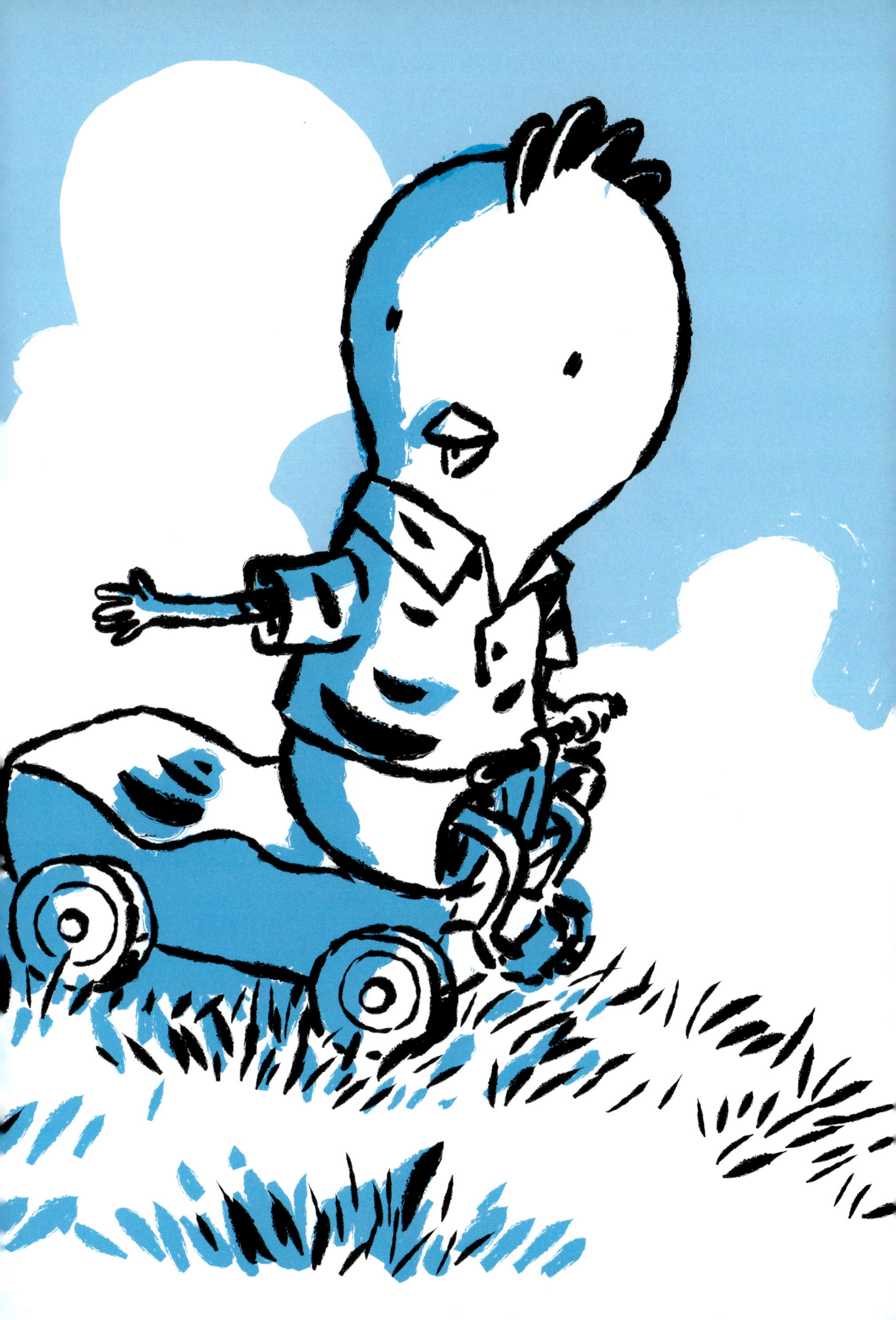

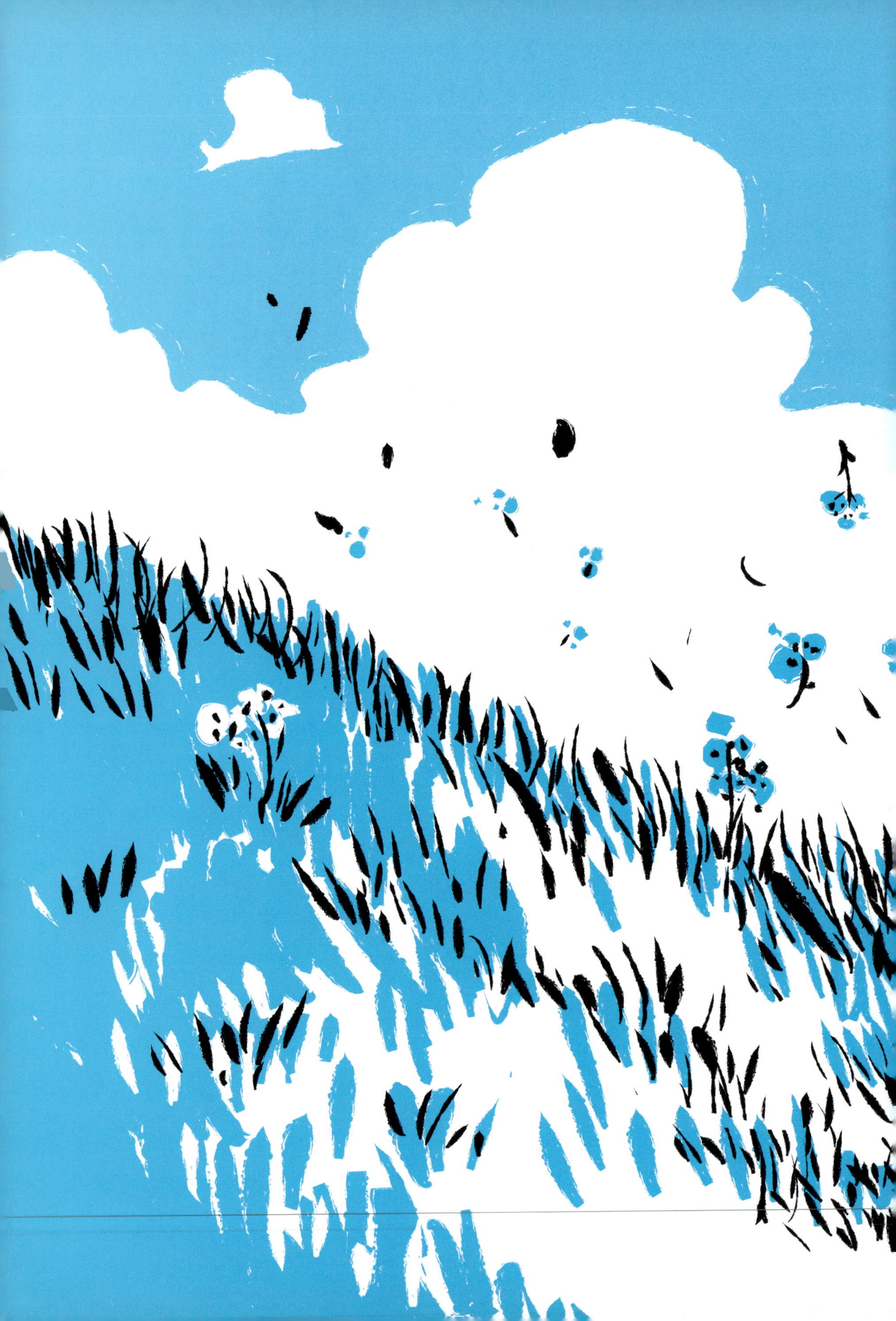

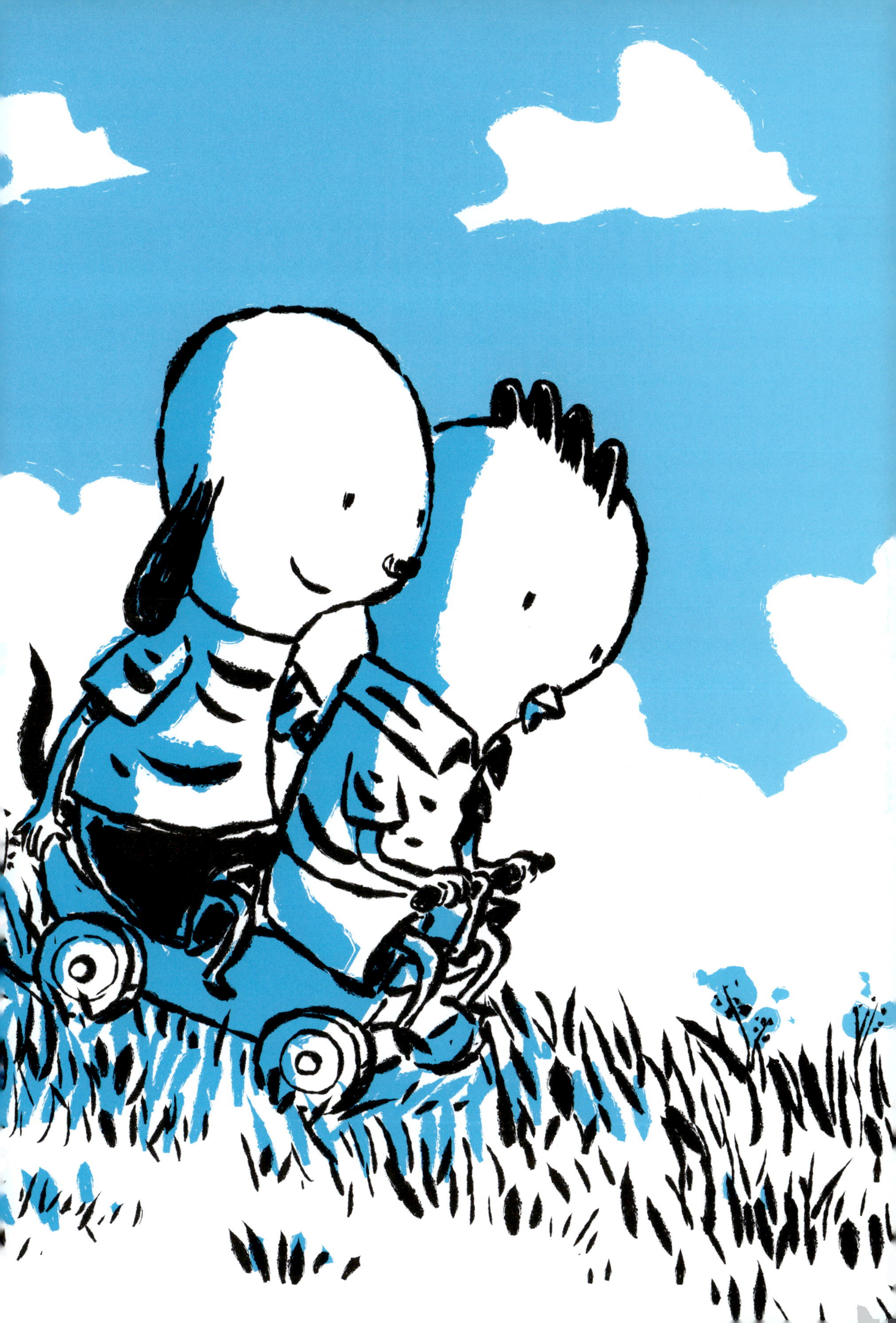

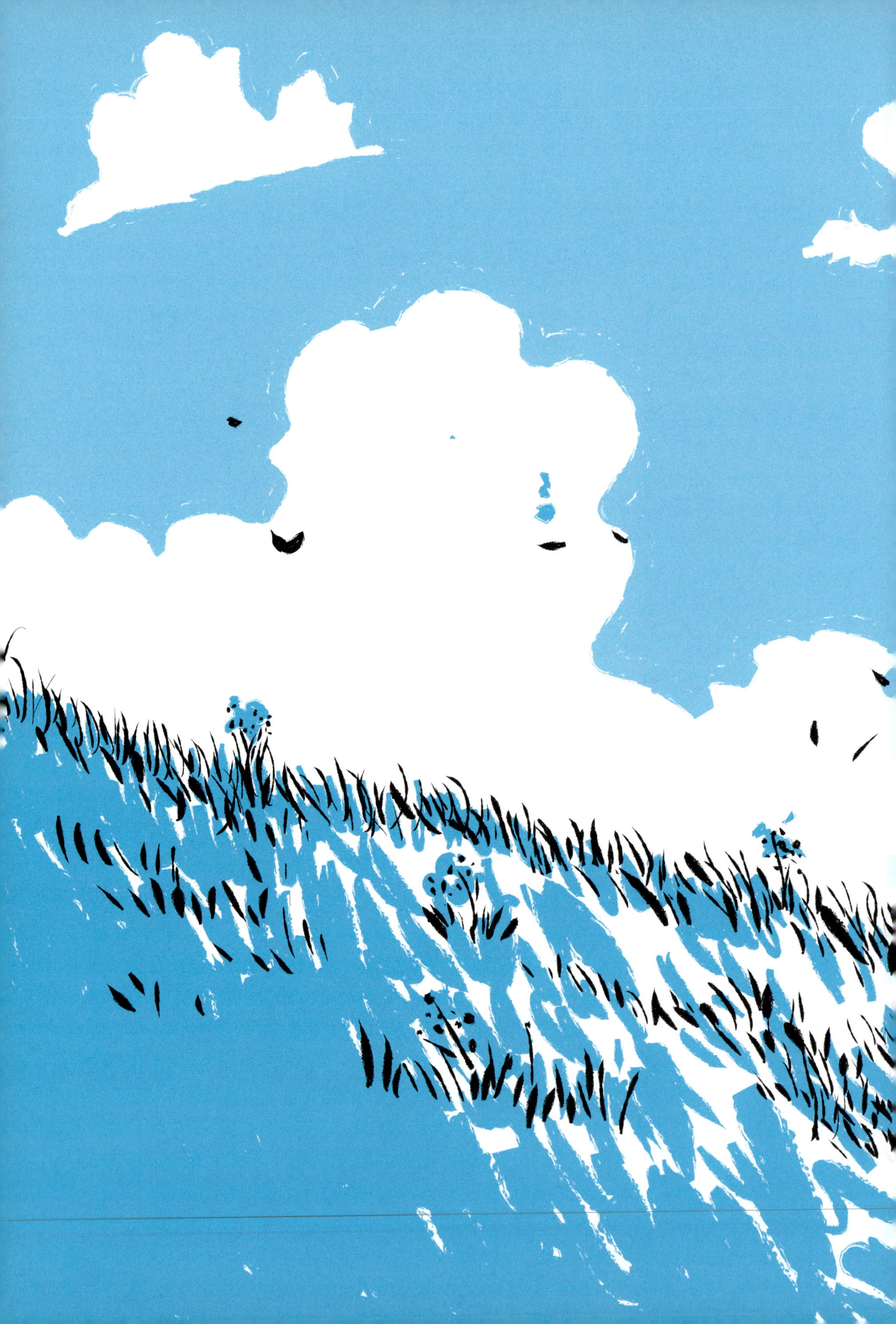

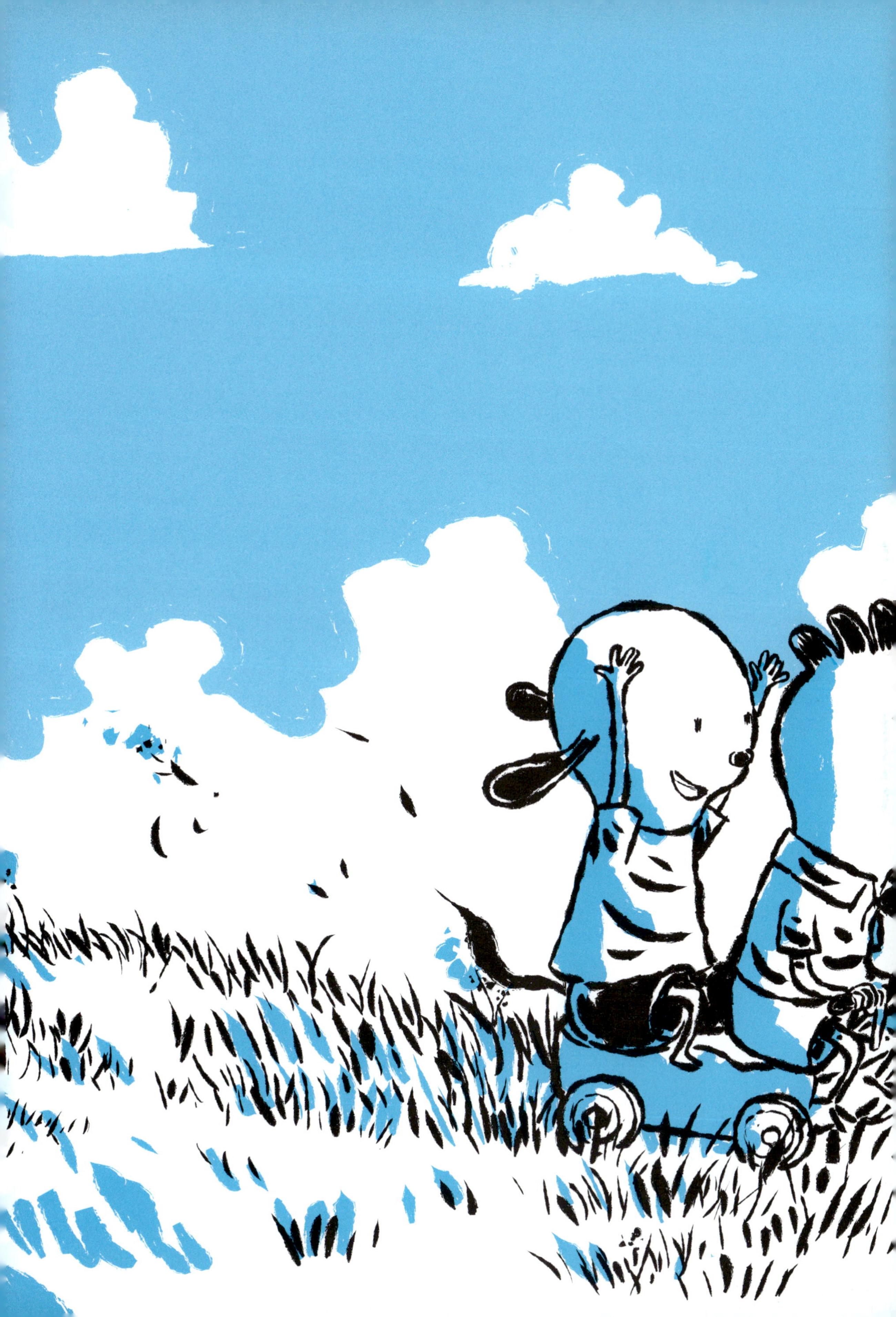

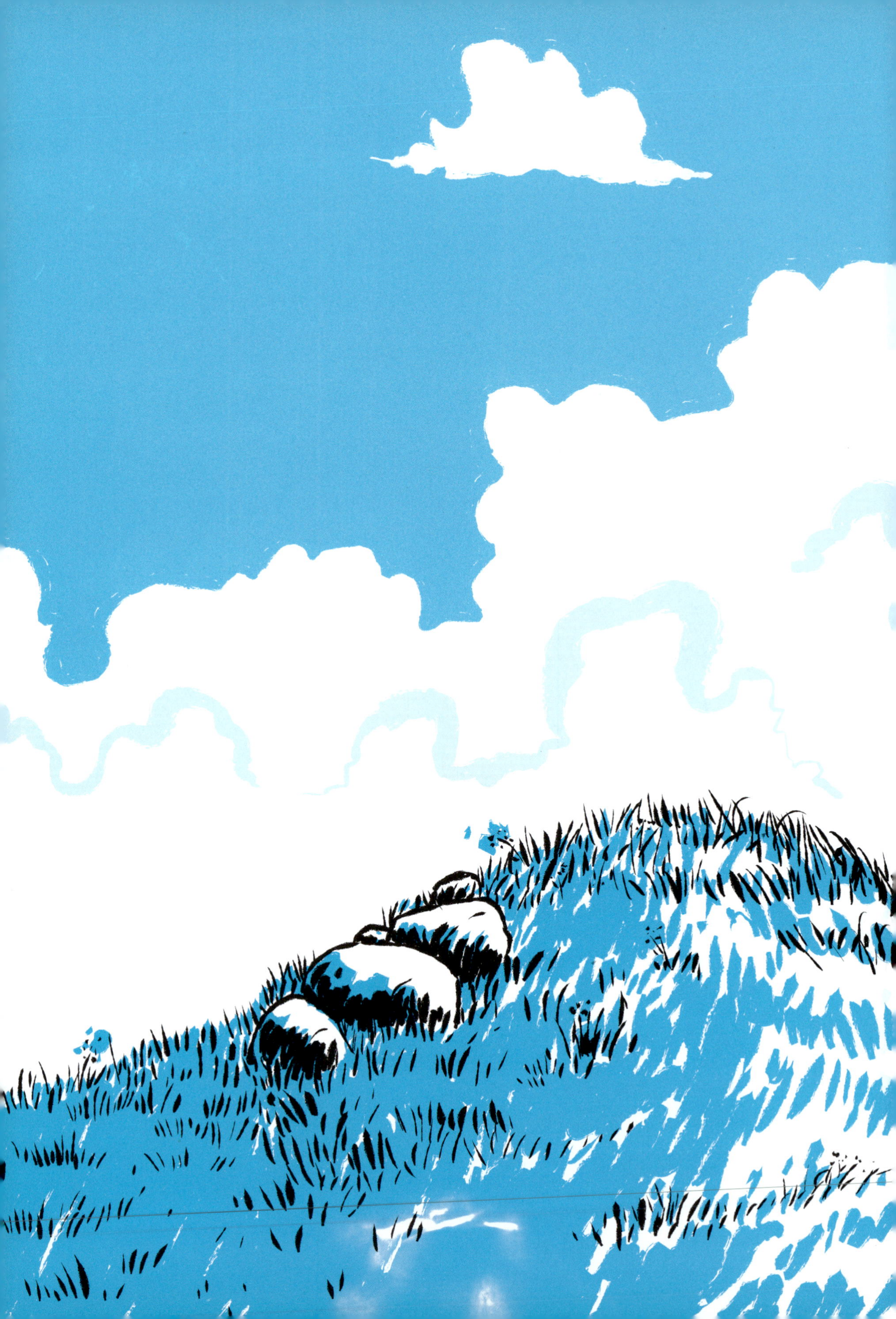

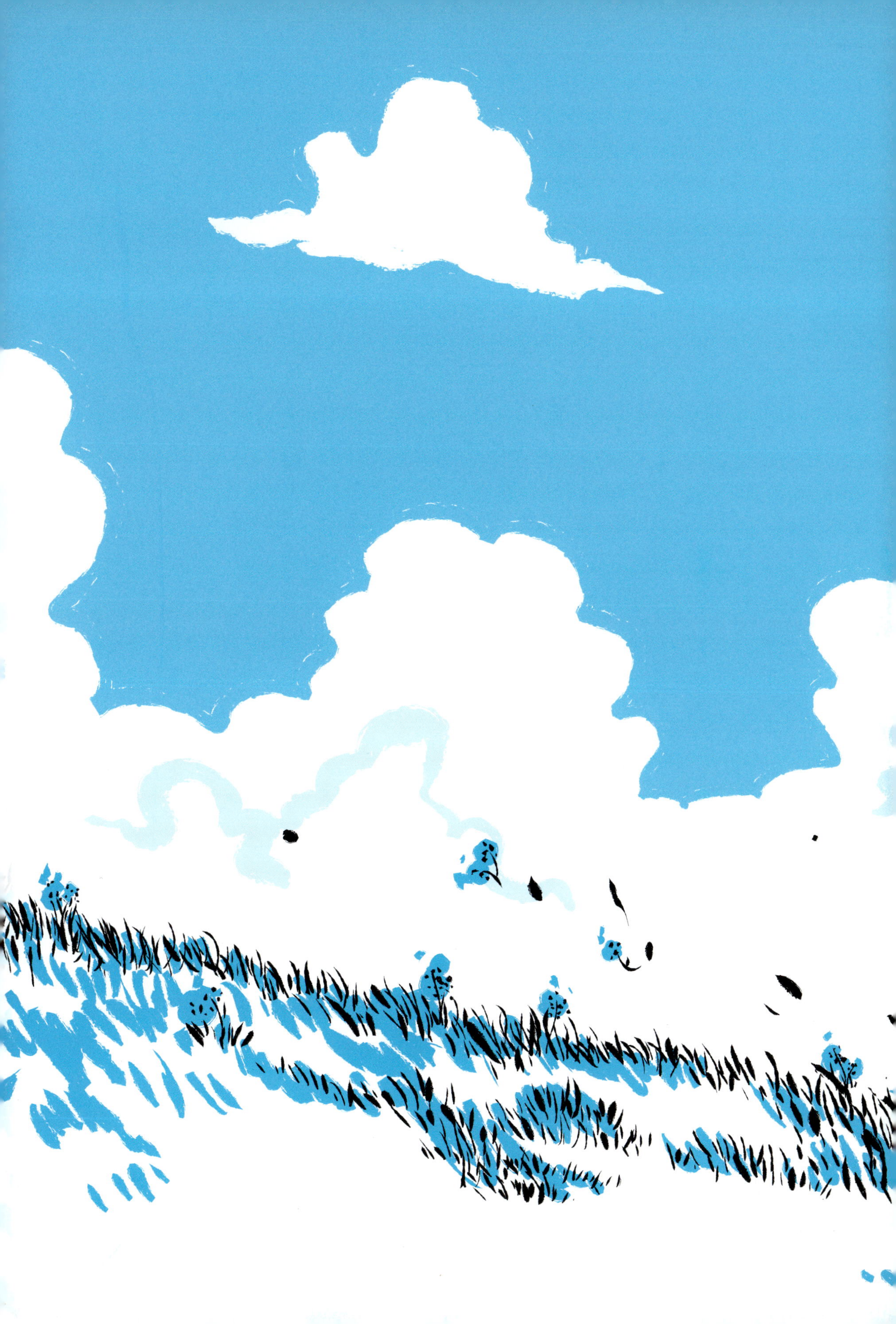

# A DIFFICULT THING
## THE IMPORTANCE OF ADMITTING MISTAKES

by Silvia Vecchini (Author), Sualzo (Artist)

Discussion Guide by **Moni Barrette, MLIS, of Creators, Assemble! Inc.**

## SYNOPSIS

Admitting you are wrong is never easy, but the ability to recognize mistakes and take responsibility is a critical social-emotional life skill. This (almost) wordless book simply yet elegantly explores how it feels to mess up and seek to make it right. Dog retrieves a wheel he broke off of Chicken's wagon but must face a scary mountain and heavy winds to bring the wheel back. Once Dog owns up to the challenge, he is forgiven, and childhood friendship is restored.

## CHARACTERS

"Dog" (unnamed protagonist), "Chicken" (unnamed friend)

## THEMES

Social-emotional learning, guilt, anxiety, relief, friendship, cooperation

## SUGGESTED AGES

Interest level, ages 4-8 years
Reading level, grades Pre-K-2

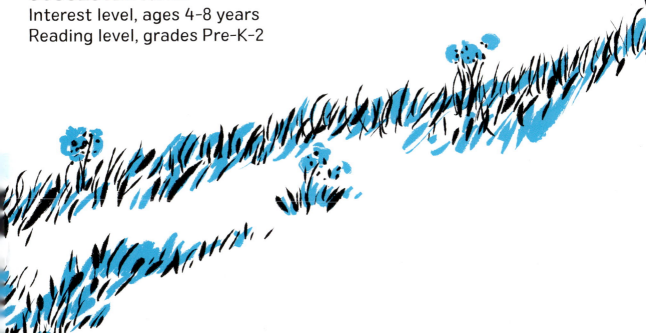

## DISCUSSION QUESTIONS

1. This story is told almost entirely through illustrations. How did the colors make you feel, and what were they trying to "say?"
2. Discuss your thoughts on the landscape (grass, leaves, clouds). Did that add to the story?
3. Many times, looking at a person's face can teach you more about how they feel than words can. How did Dog's feelings change from the beginning to the end of the story? How can you tell they changed?
4. We see Dog climbing a mountain against heavy wind, but later learn it was only a hill. Why did the author and illustrator choose to make Dog's climb look so steep? Does this have anything to do with how the character is feeling at that time?
5. Talk about a time when either you or a friend did something wrong and had to say sorry. Was it hard to admit the mistake? What did you learn from the experience?
6. Why do you think this is the only word in the story? Would it be a better story if there were more words, or is there something special about it the way that it is?

## ACTIVITY GUIDE

- CREATE

Use this template (or create your own) to draw your story. Make sure to plan the story before you start. You can make it wordless or write in the balloons.

Need prompts? Think about a time when you felt like Dog or Chicken and then draw your story.

- IMAGINE

Grab a friend and act out a scene: Pretend you did something to hurt your friend's feelings. What should you do about it? How did you feel? Take turns with the pretend roles and talk about how you both felt and what you learned.

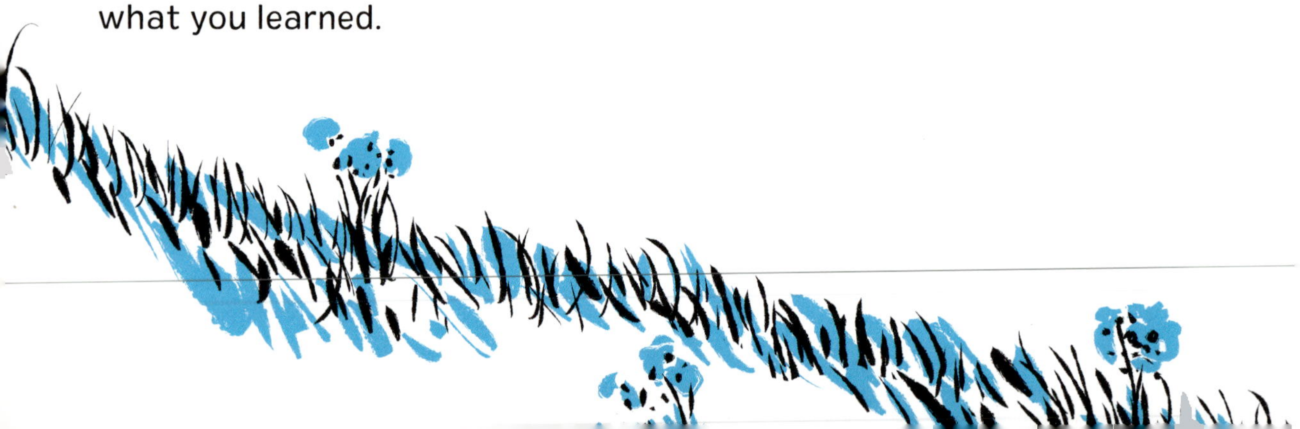

# YOUR TITLE

## ILLUSTRATION SET